GHOSTS, PIES, & ALIBIS

AMANDA REID

ENCHANTED ROCK PUBLISHING, LLC

Copyright © 2019 by Amanda Reid

All rights reserved.

No part of this book may be reproduced in any form or by any electronic or mechanical means, including information storage and retrieval systems, without written permission from the author, except for the use of brief quotations in a book review.

Cover Art by Book Cover Insanity, at bookcoverinsanity.com.

Published by Enchanted Rock Publishing, LLC

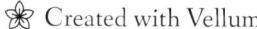 Created with Vellum

For my Family. No really. I mean it. They've been great. Putting up with my crazy questions, sequestering myself in my writing cave for hours on end, blathering incessantly about plot and characterization and motive and formatting and back cover copy and market and...well, you get the picture. Love to all of them for putting up with this author!

ONE

Mina Flannigan Shaffer slid three Cowboy Breakfasts and a Western Omelet on the pass-through ledge and tapped the silver bell. "Five's up, Rageena."

The sassy, blue-haired woman sauntered up to the window, then took a quick glance over her shoulder to the men who'd ordered the meals, the fourth unusually absent. "Wonder where OP is today?"

Mina shrugged. "No idea. I have a plate ready for him, but..." It wasn't like the Morning Boys patriarch to miss his Tuesday meeting where he held court. He bragged about the productivity of his Angus bulls, the weight he ran through the cattle auction, its price per pound, the hay he cut, the newest feed distribution machines he'd bought, all manner of running a ranch. OP Boyd always had the best, the newest, the most, and let everyone know it.

She put the extra plate of over-easy eggs, hash browns, grits, bacon, and a side of biscuits with cream gravy onto the side warming tray. She should just trash it. The morning rush of West Texas ranchers and businessmen reached its zenith half an hour ago. The likelihood of someone coming in for the Cowboy Breakfast in the next couple of minutes didn't exist. Yet she couldn't make herself slide the plate's contents into the can. A whisper in her mind stayed her hand. She shook her head and shut out the little voice. She didn't believe in the Flannigan Gift.

A glint through the pass-through caught her eye. A big silver pickup with dual back axels, a dark tint, and the battered body of a well-used ranch vehicle pulled into the slanted parking space everyone left open for OP. She pushed up to her tennis-shoed tiptoes to get a better look. At least the Morning Boys wouldn't have to hear about someone parking in his spot for half the breakfast.

The driver's door opened. Out stepped OP, adjusting the straw cowboy hat he wore during the summer. Why he bothered when he'd take it off again entering the diner mystified her, just about as much as where his two-year old, enormous extended cab, black Ford F-350 truck had gone. It was his pride and joy. But she was sure the whole diner would hear all about it.

The bell over the door tinkled. Boot thumps and a booming, "Mornin' Boys," followed by a nearly synchronized chorus of "Mornin', OP" echoed through the small opening. He took his usual spot at table five where he could see the entire diner and they could hear his booming baritone. Rageena scurried over with her coffee pot to fill his cup.

"Order up." Mina slid the Cowboy Breakfast plate she'd prepared for him onto the service ledge with a shiver traveling down her back. Of course, she hadn't known to hold onto it because she'd foreseen him arriving late. Granma would've said it was the Flannigan Gift in action. *As if*.

She glanced to the pickup, then to the empty ticket wheel. Curiosity pushed her through the swinging door from the kitchen and into the dining area. She snagged a full coffee pot and went over to the table to fill cups. "Mornin' OP, wouldn't have recognized you in the pickup," she said during a lull in the conversation.

Light flags of color appeared on the older man's weathered cheeks. "My truck wouldn't start this morning. Gonna trade it in. Cut the weak calf from the herd, right fellas?" He looked around to his three companions, who returned his announcement with nods and murmurs of "Smart," or "That's right." OP narrowed his eyes, deep set in their rheumy folds saying he had one too many bourbons every night, no doubt annoyed she'd dare to bring up his beater pickup. "Why are you behind the counter, today little lady? Haven't filled Wayne Beedy's spot yet, eh?"

The dig hit its target, but she kept her cool. She bit back the snarky comment hovering on her lips. New Mina, remember? "Sure did," she said with a smile sweeter than her cafe's legendary sweet tea. "But I told Clara to take the morning off. She's been working hard lately. I think a happy employee is a good employee, doncha think?" She looked the mean old man dead in the eye with a smile as saccharine as the ubiquitous tiny pink-packaged sweetener.

The red spots brightened to the color of his suspenders. He was notorious for being a jerk boss and barely could keep ranch hands. He hemmed and hawed before changing the subject and ignoring her completely.

With a small smile, she went back to the kitchen and readied for lunch service until Clara came through the back door, tucking her keys in her pocketbook. "Hi, boss. Thanks for the morning off." She slung an apron around her neck and tied the long strings around her ample waist. "Looks like you got me set up."

A little glow popped into Mina's heart at the cook's praise. "Learned from the best." She'd bought the Tea Cup Cafe two years ago and with Clara's direction, helped build the renamed Sweetie's Tea Cup Cafe into Dew Drop's culinary pride and joy, with a regionally-recognized chicken fried steak, one of the holy grails of Texas cuisine. The only other competition was a barbecue joint and two fast food outlets, one of which stationed itself in the Walmart.

The lunch crowd started as a trickle, then grew to a steady stream. She and her staff moved like clockwork. Before she knew it, service tailed off again, as it did every day right around one o'clock. She turned away from the farthest booth with an armload of empty plates then halted in her tracks.

"For the love of all that's holy," Mina muttered to herself. Why in the world would Wayne Beedy be standing in her restaurant's entry unless he'd come to cause trouble?

Today he appeared especially strung-out. His skin had taken on the grey cast of people who aren't getting enough oxygen. Usually greasy, shoulder-length dark hair stuck out at every angle. Clothing was torn with a huge black stain right in the middle of his gray t-shirt.

He stared at Mina across the heads of the customers in the diner's seating area, his gaze unfocused, seeming a bit confused. Fabulous. For heaven's sake, he tried to poison her sister's boyfriend, a sheriff's deputy no less, in this very restaurant not three weeks ago. And now all doped up. How in the heck had he bonded out on an attempted capital murder charge?

Ugh. Before he could do something stupid, it'd be better to get Chief Ruiz started this way. She began to weave through the tables to head off Beedy and any ensuing mayhem.

"Yoo hoo! Mina, I need to talk to you about ten pies for the church picnic." Melissa Turner, the town busybody Mina called 'Nosey', waved at her from a booth near the window.

Double fabulous. All Mina needed was the gossip about Wayne nearly poisoning someone stirred up again. "I'll be right there." Hopefully she could evict Beedy before everyone noticed him. She pulled her phone from her jean's back pocket and punched 9-1-1. She swung her gaze back to the troublemaker. Her thumb halted on its way to stab the green button to connect the call.

Where'd he go?

The bell should've sounded when he left. Had she missed it over Nosey's shrill voice? She scanned the front and side windows. No Beedy. Kayla stood at the cash register rolling silverware in paper napkins. Surely the waitress would've heard him come in or seen him standing there or even leaving, but she hadn't reacted at all. It was as if Wayne Beedy had evaporated into thin air.

Like a ghost.

The creeps danced up and down her spine as the hairs on the back of her neck rose to attention. She shook it off.

Bah. No such things as ghosts.

TWO

Mina didn't have time to argue her fortune that Wayne removed himself. When the lunch rush ended she'd call Dew Drop's finest to let the Chief know of Beedy's visit, best to deal with Melissa's order now. At least she didn't seem to have noticed Wayne across the crowded cafe. That woman's tongue wagged more than the tails in a room full of happy dogs.

Twenty minutes, fifteen changes in the pie order, and Mina's promise of a donation for the church picnic's silent auction, Melissa finally left. Another twenty minutes and the lunch rush ended as if a faucet had been turned off. Finally, she had a spare moment to ask Kayla if Beedy said anything to her before he left.

"Wayne Beedy? What are you talking about?"

Kayla Porter used a disinfectant cloth to wipe down a menu at the cashier's counter. "Haven't seen him since the Iced Tea Festival and when Chief Ruiz hauled him outta here in handcuffs for tryin' to poison Cace."

"He came in about one. Stood right there." Mina jabbed her finger to the center of the small space clear of tables where customers entered and waited. "You were standing right where you are now. You mean you didn't see him?" Good grief. How unobservant could someone be?

"Nope." Kayla's lips twisted into a grin. "You *sure* you saw Wayne Beedy."

"Of course I'm sure," Mina said in a waspish tone she'd come to associate with the Old Mina, the one who had been so unhappy she'd earned the facetious nickname "Sweetie" for her sour disposition. "I guess you just didn't see him," she said in a more cheerful manner, despite the growing weight on her shoulders she couldn't quite shake.

Kayla's round shoulders shrugged under her red Tea Cup Cafe t-shirt. "Didn't see him at all. Or smell him. He usually reeked of cigarettes." She shuddered. "Gross."

Mina pivoted and stalked to the small office she'd boot-horned into an old coat closet hidden behind the cash register station. The ancient fake leather desk chair accepted her slight weight with a squeaky groan and she rocked back to stare at the acoustic tiles in the ceiling. Why had Wayne come in today? She snorted a laugh. Who knew why that man did anything? And why hadn't Chief Ruiz called her to warn her Beedy had been released?

Might as well call him now. She reached for the phone on her desk, but her eyes snagged on a yellow sticky note. Crapoly. The Cup's accountant needed the quarterly tax information. It shouldn't take but a minute. Maybe the Chief would pop in for a late lunch. She'd call her husband after that, but Garrett could wait a couple of minutes. He had his own problems with shrinkage at the store. It appeared employee-related, and he'd been working with his dad to try to figure it out. Since nothing happened with Beedy, she'd bother her husband later. She couldn't afford a tangle with the IRS.

A malfunctioning printer-scanner caused that short minute to turn into over an hour struggling with tax forms and receipts. Finally, around two o'clock, she finished. *Almost as bad as dealing with the police paperwork when Wayne tried to poison Sunny's boyfriend. Wait. Police... Dang it.*

She dialed the number she'd saved in her phone.

Verna Mayberry answered on the very first ring. "Dew Drop Police."

Must be a slow day if she picked up that quick. "It's Mina. Is the Chief in?"

She dropped the formal tone. "Oh hey, Mina. How are you doing?"

They'd gone to school around the same time, Verna being one year behind her. Impatience rose to the surface with the need for social niceties when she had a litany of things to do, but she tamped it down. *That's the Old Mina, remember?* "Fine. I need to talk to the Chief for a second."

"He's not—wait. There he is. Hold, please." Mina didn't have enough time to figure out what popular country song the easy-listening tune once had been before Verna returned. "I'll patch you through."

"Mina?" Daniel Ruiz's deep voice boomed through the line. "I'm glad you called. I was going to come see you and grab a late lunch."

A fine tremor trilled through her, but she shook it off as she had for decades. "What's up?"

"I'll tell you when I get there."

"I can have Clara start on your chicken-fried steak if you want."

"Sure. I'll be there in ten."

She hung up and swiveled in her chair for a moment to reflect on the urgency in his tone. Usually, he made her laugh with at least one joke, sarcastic comment, or snark. The shiver returned, bringing cousins until it became an ominous foreboding. She stretched her shoulders, rotating them, trying to rid herself of the weight continuing to grow in her mind. He wouldn't bring good news.

It sounded like something Granma would say, and Mina laughed, shaking off the dark mantle, this time succeeding. Like she believed in the Flannigan Gift. Let her sisters think Granma spoke to them or they could see the future, or find things. She was smarter than that, right?

Right. She bounced out of the chair and put the Chief's order on the wheel.

Granma always told Mina not to get between a hungry man and his meal. And if Chief Daniel Ruiz hadn't eaten lunch by after two in the afternoon, he'd be hungry, so Mina had let him finish, mashed potatoes, black-eyed peas and all while she puttered around the diner, returning when he'd nearly finished.

Daniel set his fork on the virtually empty plate and slid it a bit forward. "Best chicken fried steak for four counties. My complements to Clara." He dabbed at his mouth and the impressive salt and pepper moustache. With a level assessment of Mina who sat across from him in the booth, he folded his arms and rested them on the table. "Why don't you tell me why you called."

"I thought you might want to know Wayne Beedy must've made bond. He came in about one, but before I could get to him, he left. He looked weird, like he was on drugs or something."

Chief Ruiz's eyes narrowed to laser points and his jaw set. "Wayne Beedy was *here*." He tapped his blunt index finger on the table with each word. "In Sweetie's Tea Cup Cafe?"

"Yeah. Here."

He ran his hand over his short, black hair to rub the back of his neck. "Jesus, Mina. Why didn't you call us earlier?"

"It was in the middle of lunch and we were busy today. I called when I had time. I thought he'd cause some trouble, but he left. I also thought you'd want to know he was probably back on drugs."

No trace of the usual humor filled his features. "Wayne Beedy didn't get out on bond. He escaped last night."

THREE

It took several moments for the Chief's words to sink in, but Mina still had to confirm she'd heard right. "Escaped."

He nodded. "He'd been in Eastland County Jail enough times, they pretty much had a jumpsuit with his name embroidered on it. He'd been a trustee in the past, so..." He shook his head.

"You mean they let him outside the jail clean up trash? Even with what he did to Cace?" The guy had been charged with attempted murder of a police officer for goodness sake.

"He was washing squad cars. Let's just say the Sheriff's had some words with the person who made *that* decision." Daniel's lips twisted. "I'd been out all morning at his usual haunts around town—mamma, grandma, babies' mamma's houses plus his usual dealer friends—and he wasn't there. I flat can't believe he'd be stupid enough to come in here."

"I know, right? But he stood right in front of Kayla, not ten feet away, and she said she didn't see him. Didn't even say anything to her." Mina shrugged. "He looked confused. That's why I thought he was on drugs. Usually, he's mean as a rabid wasp. If I hadn't been desperate, I'd never have hired him during the Iced Tea Festival." She shredded herself mentally for the hundredth time.

"If you see him again, call 9-1-1 immediately. Don't wait. They want him back pretty bad, so they've put extra deputies in this part of the county." He grabbed his pristine straw cowboy hat from the seat next to him and stood, looking down at her from his six-foot height. "How much for the chicken fried steak?"

"I'll put it on your bill."

The corners of his eyes crinkled at the usual response to his question. "I better let the Sheriff know Beedy's been in town. He's had to call in the Texas Rangers with the escape, but I don't know if they've arrived yet." Daniel turned, then pivoted back. "Do you have a surveillance system?"

"No. Been meaning to put one in since last month." It went without saying Wayne had been the catalyst for the idea so she could monitor everything in real time. It moved to the top of her honey-do list.

"See you do. With him on the loose, you'll want to make sure you lock your doors. I don't think he liked being in jail again, and he may come back to make trouble for you. Let your staff know. And make sure you tell Garrett to be on the lookout, okay?"

"Geez, Daniel. Of course I'll tell my husband." She batted her eyelashes at him to emphasize the sarcasm.

It earned her a quirk of his wiry brow. "You're a little too independent sometimes, missy."

She mock-bristled. "Missy? How old are you, Methuselah?"

"I'm as old as your daddy. So, you better mind." With the parting shot, he wheeled and strode down the aisle, boot heels heavy on the tile floor.

"Humph." She grabbed his plate and glass, took them through the swinging service door into the kitchen. Her eye snagged the clock. Almost three.

Dang it. Late again. She added the plate to the pile next to Clara, who stood rinsing dishes and loading them in the washer. "I've got to run and pick up Jake. Are you good to hold it down until then? Rageena's here for another half hour."

Dimples appeared in the cheeks of the older woman's cherubic face. "It's slower 'n molasses around here. Go on and get your son. I'll be here 'til you get back."

"Thanks. Did you hear Wayne Beedy escaped from Eastland Jail? He was here earlier, so be on the lookout."

The dish Clara held slipped onto the floor and shattered.

For a moment, the they both stared at the stoneware shards. As if prodded by the same stick, they both turned toward the cleaning closet.

Clara waved her off. "I've got it, Mina. Go get your boy."

"Who dropped the dish?" Rageena Walton's face popped in the serving window. Her eager, heavily blue-eyeshadowed eyes took in the scene. "Clara? Aw, man."

In order to keep expenses down, Mina had made a game of betting who would be the next to break a plate. Clara almost never dropped one. Everyone, including Mina, chipped in five bucks and couldn't bet on themselves to keep the competition fair. Clara hadn't dropped one since Mina took over the diner, and her name never appeared on anyone's guess.

"Pot gets richer," Mina said. "I'll put a note on the board to make sure everyone gets their bets and money in the envelope by their next shift. Gotta run."

Halfway to Dew Drop Elementary, the phone she'd left in her back jeans pocket vibrated. She tugged it out. Garrett. *Shoot.* She should've called him.

"Hi honey." She winced at the fake chipper tone.

"You on your way to pick up Jake?" How well he knew her. And how well he knew she was always running late.

"Yep. Almost there."

"Okay, anything *else* you need to tell me?"

Ugh. She'd gotten used to trying to manage everything in her life, including her husband, he'd think she deliberately hadn't told him. But with their recent reunion after a separation, she swore to turn over a new leaf and let him share the load. Plus, he'd be worried if Beedy came in. "I was going to call you but we got busy. Who'd you hear it from?"

He chuckled. "Kayla came for some duct tape after her shift. Said you saw Wayne in the Cup."

Thanks, Kayla. "It was weird. He came in then left right away. I told Daniel." She relayed her conversation with the Chief to her husband.

All traces of Garrett's earlier humor evaporated. "I'm glad you called him. We'll get the security system installed at the house and the Cup this week." They'd been talking about it for a while, but one of his assistant managers recently quit and he'd picked up the extra shifts at the family business, Shaffer Hardware, three blocks down the street from her cafe. The extra hours and the employee theft had decimated his time.

"I'm getting ready to hit the school zone. We'll talk tonight." They said their goodbyes. She managed to put the phone in the center console before she got to the school zone's flashing yellow lights. She slowed to the requisite speed, then pulled into the pickup line. At least she'd made it early enough that Jake didn't have to wait alone. She'd been trying hard lately. Getting back together with Garrett and having someone to share the load with helped. Good grief. *Allowing* someone to share the load was more like it.

She scanned the throng of kids and tooted her horn—*beep, beep, beep*—when she saw Jake.

He grabbed his backpack and slung it over his shoulder. Instead of his usual trot to the SUV he strolled toward her, away from the girl he'd been talking to. He climbed in and dropped his book bag on the floorboard.

"Hey buddy, how was school?"

"Huh?" He turned from looking out the window, away from staring at the young blonde smiling at him with a sly curl way beyond her years.

For heaven's sake, he's only in second grade. She

sighed. Garrett started bugging her in third grade, no real difference. A horn behind Mina prompted her to move along. She turned back onto Live Oak Street, back toward downtown at the sedate pace posted.

"Who were you talking to? I don't recognize her."

"Kinley Majors. She's new."

Where had she heard that name? Ah, yes. Clara's grandniece. Interesting how her normally introverted son had been chatty with the girl, but now had less than normal to say. She turned her head to Jake, taking in his stillness. "She's pretty."

He shifted. "Uh...yeah." His cheeks flooded bright red, but he stubbornly kept his eyes trained forward through the windshield.

Shoot fire. She was *not* ready for her little boy to be in puppy love. She turned her attention back to the road.

Wayne Beedy stood in the middle of her lane.

FOUR

Mina screamed and yanked the wheel to the right. Jammed on her breaks then came to a stop on the shoulder in a skid of gravel. She whipped a glance over her left shoulder, but Beedy disappeared again. Where had he gone? There hadn't been a thump as she rolled over his body. Had there? Her pulse kicked up to heart attack level.

Heavy breathing to her right brought her back to Jake. "You okay, buddy?"

"Yeah," he squeaked, eyes wide.

"I'll be right back." She didn't want to go look. Would've rather driven off and pretended she hadn't just run over the man. A couple of deep breaths calmed her shaking hands enough to open the door and slide out onto the blazing hot pavement. No body lay in the middle of the street. She scanned behind her truck. Skid marks from her tires led onto the shoulder. No blood. No body on either side of the road. She peeped into the bed of her pickup. Nope. Then... Bile burned in her throat and she steadied her herself with a hand to the tailgate. *Just look.* She counted to three and crouched down.

No mangled Wayne.

Mina shot up. Raced to the front of her truck. No dent, no blood. No indication she'd hit anyone. But...she had to have hit him. He couldn't have been but ten feet in front of the truck when she'd noticed him.

The blast of a horn startled her so much, she should've been hanging from the moon. Mina grabbed at the t-shirt over her hammering heart. A familiar white SUV had pulled up beside her with the passenger window rolled down. From inside, Olivia Summers asked, "You okay?"

Mina checked the snarky comment hovering on her lips and moved toward the vehicle. She stepped up onto the running board to peer inside. Blessed cool air blew from the interior. "Yeah. I-I thought I ran over someone's dog. But I must've missed him." Why'd she lie to her best friend? Because she was going crazy, that's why.

Olivia laughed. "Oh man. Scared the heck outta myself the last time that happened. Glad you missed it. Hey, are you going to the Youth Ministry picnic this weekend? Or better question—are your pies going to be there?" Her friend's saucy gloss-rimmed smile and sarcasm about Mina's lack of regular church attendance brought a sense of normalcy she desperately needed to calm her shaky nerves.

Mina nodded. "Coconut cream and chocolate delight. I put up a pie-a-month for auction since it'll benefit the ministry's mission trip."

"I don't know how you'll keep the meringue on them in this heat—ooh." Olivia shifted sideways in her seat and propped her arm on the steering wheel. "Did you hear Wayne Beedy escaped from Eastland County Jail?"

Sweat slid between Mina's breasts, and not only from the early-September Texas heat. "Yeah." She had no desire to discuss the subject. Mina pulled at the front of her Tea Cup logo t-shirt a couple times to cool a bit. "I've got to get back to the cafe."

"Sure, Sweetie. See you soon."

Mina gave a little wave and climbed in her pickup as Olivia drove off. The last couple of weeks Mina had come to hate the nickname. She'd earned it with pride over her thirty years, how could she change it now? It even graced the official title of her restaurant. But who cared about a stupid nickname when Wayne Beedy seemed intent on haunting her every step today? Where had he gone? And where would he pop up next?

"Mom? Why'd we stop?"

Good lord, she'd forgotten Jake. She considered giving him the same dog story she'd spouted to Olivia, but found she couldn't lie to her son. "A man has been following me today. He was in front of the truck in the road and I thought I hit him."

His little eyebrows scrunched together. "In front of the truck? There wasn't a man in front of the truck."

"What? Of course there was, honey." He just hadn't seen him.

He studied her with solemn brown eyes. "No mom, there wasn't."

Anger started to nibble at her. As if she didn't know what she saw. *Down hotheaded Sweetie.* "Okay, buddy, maybe I just imagined him." She patted his skinny knee. Something struck a chord. Unwelcome memories welled up. Children pointing and laughing at her on a playground. In a schoolroom. At church. She shook her head like it would clear the images. Maybe Jake had it right and it had been a figment of Beedy's earlier visit. Stress. Stress had her imagining him. She hadn't had a vacation in two years.

GHOSTS, PIES, & ALIBIS 25

Jake sighed and looked out the passenger window. "You didn't imagine him. It was a ghost."

The blood in her veins turned to ice. "What are you talking about? There's no such thing as ghosts." While the words emerged from her mouth, a part of her nodded in agreement with her son. What? *No. There. Are Not.* Ghosts don't exist. They can't. *They can't.*

"His hair stuck out everywhere. He had a gray t-shirt with a big stain in the middle. They all look gray. Always gray," he whispered.

Holy balls of fire. Beedy. How...? Chills prickled her skin. Her child saw ghosts? She cleared her throat. "Sweetheart—" Words failed her. There were no such things as ghosts. No paranormal world. No Flannigan Gift. Granma claimed to have it. Said all of the girls in the family had a version of some psychic ability. Lacey supposedly got the full monty of visions like Granma. Sunny said she found things needing to be returned to their owners. Total load of crap.

Right? Yes. It had to be yes.

"Granma said you used to see ghosts, but then kids at school used to make fun of you. So, you stopped." He pivoted his head and the depth in his eyes stunned her. "She said I shouldn't tell people I see ghosts because they wouldn't understand and get mad or they'd make fun of me."

Her heart dropped into the yawing pit which had grown in her stomach. He didn't tell his mother. Couldn't tell her? "Granma told you not to tell people you see ghosts?"

He looked down at his clasped hands. "Lacey knows."

Lacey? Her own sister? And she didn't tell Mina? "Why didn't you tell me?" She struggled to keep the tears she'd pushed back from her tone.

"Granma said it would make you mad and you'd want me to stop seeing them."

Her heart tore in two, anger that Granma told Mina's own son to hide something from her, and sorrow he felt he couldn't tell her. She wanted to rage at Granma, but Mina would have to wait until she visited her grave.

"Does Dad know?" She forced a lid on her roiling emotions. If Garrett knew, she'd explode.

"No." His voice had faded with each previous answer until she had to struggle to hear the denial.

She moderated her tone. "Jake, sweetheart, look at me." The anguish swimming with his brimming tears destroyed her anger. Her child struggled and he hadn't felt able to talk to her or Garrett about it. "I'm not mad. I believe you. And I'm sorry you felt you couldn't tell me."

By all that's holy, had she, Mina Flannigan, great denier of the Flannigan Gift and anything paranormal, admitted she believed her son saw ghosts?

The implication blindsided her in a sneaky rush.

If Jake saw ghosts, so did she.

FIVE

Mina sat in Granma's favorite oversized chintz chair in the darkened front parlor. Emotions tumbled through her as she stared through the enormous bay window at the shifting shadows in the deep, shaded edges of their yard.

A ghost. She saw Wayne Beedy's *spirit*. She couldn't deny it any longer. Old Mina would've snorted then made a mean, snarky comment about the stupidity of people who believed in such bull-fertilizer. The certainty sitting in Mina's gut now said Jake spoke the truth. Well, her gut *and* the memories she'd kept long suppressed which had come first as a trickle, then a rush, like they competed to be released from their prison.

She'd had several hours to examine them, pull them, push them, poke them, call them baloney, but

GHOSTS, PIES, & ALIBIS   29

she hadn't imagined the scenes. And it left her...terrified. Not of the ghosts. Of her ability to lie to herself for decades. And of how horribly she'd treated her Granma and sisters all these years. The Flannigan Gift. If Mina could see ghosts, then it was real.

A subtle laughter echoed in her mind, reminding her of Granma. Maureen Flannigan certainly would've found it amusing her stubborn eldest granddaughter now believed. And if Mina could see ghosts, and Granma had visions, it meant she had to believe in both Sunny's and Lacey's powers, too.

Sorrow mixed with longing filled Mina. If she could only talk to Granma, now it was too late. But she could talk to her sisters. And she'd do it tomorrow. After ten on a work night didn't make for a good time for apologies.

Through the window, a dark shape detached itself from the shadows in the yard. Her breathing hitched. Another ghost? Wayne Beedy? Or someone else? The shape fell to all fours. Too small for a human. A distinctive waddle moved its rotund form from side to side as it crossed the yard toward the alley. Ah. Her breathing returned to normal. A raccoon. *Reminder—have Garrett set some live traps in the shed, garage and attic.* Those cute little monsters wreaked havoc in old homes.

She laughed at the momentary fright the varmint

caused. Who knew Mina Flannigan Shaffer would jump at any little shadow? A little voice in her head snorted a laugh. *Who knew she would believe in the Flannigan Gift?*

The fundamental change in her viewpoint still perched uneasily in her mind. And not only because of what it meant for her.

Footsteps on the stairs drew her attention from her troubled thoughts. Too heavy for Jake. She'd wanted some time to speak to him, ask him how he experienced his version of the Gift, but there hadn't been time. Between dinner and homework, it had been bedtime. And Garrett had been home. There just hadn't been a right moment to continue the conversation.

"What's going on?" Garrett's tone carried concern.

How could she explain... Her mouth went dry.

He pushed away from where he'd propped his shoulder on the cased opening hiding the pocket doors, then moved further into the room until he stood before her, his visage an outline against the bare moonlight through the windows. After ten years of marriage, how could she tell him she saw ghosts, let alone their son did, too?

She scanned up, past the baggy pajama bottoms

hugging his hips, up his bare, muscled chest to his face, lined with concern.

"Uh oh." He reached beside her and switched on the side table's lamp, then crouched down and took her hands. "What's wrong?"

Her lip trembled. How would he handle the news? He didn't believe in the Flannigan Gift either. "You have to promise not to get mad." She pushed the hated tears back.

"Of course I won't." His hands tightened a bit around hers, a silent encouragement.

Stalling wouldn't help. She needed to rip the band-aid, as Granma used to say. A sudden agitation strummed her nerves and she needed to move to dispel the energy. She disengaged herself and slid around him to begin pacing the length of the parlor, to the opening, to the darkened fireplace, then back.

"That bad?" He'd taken her spot in Granma's chair.

She stopped and faced him. "It's about me. And Jake."

"Okay." His features set carefully to neutral.

"There's something you need to know. Something I recently discovered. I should've known it all along, but I was too stubborn to admit it." She threw up her hands and started pacing again.

"Stubborn *is* your middle name."

"Ha, ha. It's Flannigan, in case you forgot. And it's what this is about." What would he say if she told him?

"Good, because I was beginning to worry you'd tell me Jake wasn't my child."

"What?" The screeched word echoed off the polished hardwood floor. She lowered her tone since Jake was in bed. "You don't believe that."

He huffed a laugh. "No. But you've never had trouble telling me exactly what you're thinking. I thought it might shake something loose."

She wagged a finger. "One of these days, Garrett Roy Shaffer..." But she merely delayed. *In for a penny, in for a pound.* Another of Granma's old sayings. "I can see ghosts." There. She'd said it.

He didn't move a muscle. Twitch. Smile. Raise his eyebrows. Nothing.

The lack of reaction from her husband began to unnerve her. Seconds stretched into an eternity until she couldn't take it any longer. "Say something."

"Of all the things you could've said, that's probably the last thing I'd have thought."

"I know, right?" She swung around and resumed pacing. "Who knew Mina Flannigan Shaffer would ever say she believed in the Flannigan Gift?"

"Now you believe in the Gift, eh?" Amusement colored his tone.

She waved a hand. "Yes. But that's not the point. The point is I see ghosts."

"What brought this on?"

"Wayne Beedy."

He straightened in the cushy wingback. "How in the world did that crook get you to believe in ghosts?"

"Because he came into the Cup today."

"So?"

She shook her head, impatient with her inability to explain this in a logical manner. *Like seeing ghosts is logical?* "I didn't see *him*. I saw his *ghost*."

"You saw his *ghost*." His tone rang with disbelief.

"Don't you see? I didn't believe then." She crossed the short distance to him. "He was gray. I thought the drugs he did might've caused a lack of oxygen in his blood or something, like Granma, when she had the heart congestion." The scene replayed in her memory. *Wait a minute.* "Only he was way grayer all over. Wow. I didn't notice it earlier. And even though he wasn't but ten feet from Kayla, she said she didn't see or hear him. Or smell him. Don't you remember you could practically smell him coming he stank so bad of cigarettes?"

"Lemme get this straight. For these reasons you think you saw his ghost in the Cup." Garrett shook his head. "Daniel said he escaped. Not that he died."

"Not for those reasons. Because I thought I ran him over after I picked up Jake from school."

"You thought you ran him over?"

Funny how people parroted your statements when they had a hard time dealing with them. "He stood right in front of me, vacant eyes staring me down. I swerved to miss him." She jammed her fists on her hips. "You think I'm crazy."

"Not crazy." She let him search for more words. "Stressed. Maybe the Cup is getting a little too much?"

She laughed. The freedom of understanding what had driven her all of these years made her feel maybe she could right her ship. "It's what I thought, too. Jake convinced me it had been Beedy's ghost."

"How in the world did he do that?" Her husband's eyebrows crawled up his forehead.

Garrett tolerated Granma and her talk about the Gift. Would he accept his son having it? She groped for the words, but found the ones hovering on her lips initially had been the simplest. "Because he sees them, too."

Garrett sat for a moment, then said, "Well, it explains a lot."

SIX

Of all the things Garrett could've said, that was the furthest from Mina's expectations. "Explains what?"

"There's this bond with him and Lacey. It seemed to get stronger when Maureen died."

She pulled back to look at him. Why hadn't she noticed the link after Granma passed? "Wait—why aren't you upset and saying he's stressed too?"

The edges of his lips curled. "You've denied the Gift for so long, I thought maybe you've been working too hard." He leaned forward in the chair and put his forearms on his thighs. He looked from side to side as if not wanting someone to overhear. "I've got a secret to tell you. I've always believed in the Gift. You're the one who's been adamant it was a hoax."

"But you always agreed..." She sputtered to a stop, mouth hanging open.

He rose, then put his hands on her shoulders, a smile gentled his face. "No, I let your statements stand."

"But..." Her whole world flipped on its axis. He wouldn't have kept that from her all these years? But he had. "Why? Why didn't you tell me?

"I always respected your Grandmother. I didn't see her as a liar or a con. She never used her Gift for gain, only to help, like when Mike Berry's son walked away from their ranch house ten years ago. She told them where to look and they found him on a day when sub-freezing temperatures could've killed that three-year old."

"I'd always thought it was luck..." The guilt, the shame of all of the years overcame her. Her grandmother had saved that child. And all Mina had ever done was ridicule the Gift.

"You were still at college and I was helping the whole town to search for him. I heard her say to look in the old corn crib on the far side of the place. No one thought he could've made it very far. Almost two miles from the house through some pretty thick scrub. Yet...we found him there." His voice carried wonder. "People may make fun of the Flannigans, but they never discounted what

Garrett said with a wry twist to his lips. "Who would've wanted the guy dead?"

She half-snorted a laugh. "I'm sure there's a line a mile long. Dope dealers he might have stiffed. People he's stolen from. Three kids from a couple of different relationships?"

"It was a rhetorical question, but I agree, the list must be lengthy."

She flopped into Granma's chair and massaged her tired eyes with her fingers. "Of course he'd come back to cause me trouble. If only Clara's dad hadn't gotten sick right at the Festival. I'd never have had to rely on him. Do you think he's coming back to haunt me because I got him arrested?"

"I'm pretty sure trying to poison Cace got him arrested and charged with attempted capital murder. If anyone, Beedy probably would haunt him instead."

The day he'd been taken out of the cafe in handcuffs he'd vowed revenge on her. All for calling the cops after he'd poisoned a deputy's food. "Oh crap. I could be on the list of people wanting to kill him—he swore he'd get me."

"No one would think you'd murder Wayne Beedy."

"Everybody in the restaurant, including danged Melissa Turner heard him threaten me." Crappity crap. "And I did say I'd shoot him if he showed up again."

Garrett rubbed his chin with his index finger. "I really don't believe people would think of you as a murderer."

She hoped so, but she couldn't help the snappy comeback. "I thought I was 'The Meanest Girl West of the Mississippi'."

"But you're working on that." His eyes raked her body with blatant suggestion. "In fact, why don't we work on it together right now? Upstairs...in bed."

Her cheeks blazed. "I...ah..."

He smirked. "Take your time. I'll be upstairs waiting for you. And you were a bad girl for not calling me earlier. Remember that." His low laugh followed him out of the parlor.

Mina closed her eyes. Her hands rubbed at the heat roaring in her cheeks.

"I thought he'd never leave," a male voice said.

If her heart could've jumped out of her chest and run for cover, it would've. Her eyes popped open on a smothered screech.

Wayne Beedy sat on the couch opposite her.

SEVEN

Mina clutched her t-shirt above her racing heart. "Geezus. How did you get in here?"

"You *can* see me." His words carried satisfaction but also a bit of shock.

"Yes," she snapped in a whisper. What if Garrett heard her talking to herself? "I can see you. What I want to see is your butt headed out the door. Or through the wall or however you ghosts leave."

Wayne made no move to skedaddle.

There had to be a way to make him leave her house. She concentrated hard, willed him to begone. Several seconds later, she cracked open an eye in the silence. She launched to her feet and pointed a finger in the direction of the window. "You heard what I said, get out. Shoo. Leave. I don't know how more plain I can make it."

His jaw firmed under its scrabby, shadowy beard. "I'm not leaving and you can't make me. I need your help."

"Not from me you don't." Her fists balled on her hips. "If you'd wanted help, you wouldn't have tried to kill Cace in my restaurant."

"Yeah, well, he shouldn't have been so mean."

"Arresting someone for shoplifting doesn't qualify as mean."

His gaze dropped. "I had to pay some bills before some money came in." His features tightened and he swung angry eyes back to her. "And it's not like Walmart was really going to miss the stuff. It's a big company."

"Pay some bills, eh? So, your dealer sends them in the mail? Does he have a payment plan?"

Wayne crossed his arms at his scrawny chest, his mouth a tight, angry line. "You always were a witch."

"Nice. Not exactly a complement that would get me to help you."

"If you don't help me, I'll just keep showing up." He smirked.

"Ha! I don't care. Keep showing up. I can ignore you."

"Even upstairs where Garrett is waiting for you? While you're doing it I can give a running commentary..."

Oh my grits and gravy. Her cheeks burned. No way. Mina rallied. "If you think you can blackmail me into—"

"If you had seen your face when I said it, you'd know that's exactly what I *know* I can do." He snickered. His eyes, darkened to pits, evaluated her body, down then up, lingering at her chest.

Every girl in town had gotten the same look, the one that said, *I'm imagining you naked right now.* Creeps raged up and down her spine. "Fine. What do you want me to do?" She huffed a breath. "It better not be illegal."

"I want you to find out who killed me." He tugged at his stained shirt. The large blotch covered a good foot of fabric on the front and left side of his chest. A darker circular hole toward his sternum looked to be a bullet hole. Television and movies tended to show ghosts as transparent. To her they manifested as substantial as people, only grayer, like old black and white television. *Creepy*.

She shivered. "The police can look into your murder."

"No, I want you to do it."

She threw her hands up. "For heaven's sake, it's what they do for a living. I own a restaurant. I'm not a cop."

"Don'cha see?" He spread his arms wide. "They

won't care. I'm just the town doper. I've been in trouble my whole life—*was* in trouble my whole life," he corrected with a shake of his head. "I'm sure they think I've stiffed dope dealers. I've got babies everywhere and owe more support than I could ever pay back." He focused his once blue-irised gaze on her. "I could've killed Cace, a police officer. I ran away from Eastland County Jail. Like they'll even try to figure it out. They'll poke around, then dust their hands off and shrug their shoulders. I'll be some case file they move from their cabinet in a couple of years to a shelf in the storage room. Big ol' 'Unsolved' stamped on it." His bitter words carried a hefty amount of self-loathing.

Any bit of regret for uttering her earlier unkind words about Wayne was stifled by the fact he was blackmailing her. Her brows rose. "You've been watching too many true-crime shows."

"Yeah, well, what else do you have to do in jail but watch the tee-vee? Doesn't matter, you know I'm right."

Probably. Which seemed the tiniest bit unjust. He and Garret had been of age, two years ahead of her. He'd been a good kid at one time, attractive, and from a decent family. Where had it all gone wrong? Soon after graduation, his parents moved to Weatherford, a larger town between Dew Drop and Fort

Worth, but Wayne stuck around. Like he stuck around here after his death? To be up to no good?

"Why don't you tell me who killed you?" Mina suggested. "You tell me, I tell Chief Ruiz." Though how she'd explain she came to have the information would be fun.

He shifted. "I don't know who did it."

"What do you mean 'you don't know'? You *were* there, weren't you?" For the love of all that's holy, only Wayne would not know who killed him. "Can't you even guess? I mean, how many people want to kill you? Is there a line?"

A muscle twitched at his jaw. "I don't know who did it." His gaze grew distant. "I hitched a ride to town from Eastland jail. I stopped at Kasey's gas station and hung out, mostly around back in the shade. After the sunset, I started walking to Brittany's house. I think I stopped for a break at the elementary school. The next thing I know, I hear a gunshot and..." He gestured to his chest. "I turned and saw someone in a dark hoodie and jeans, but I couldn't see his face."

"Brittany who? The only one I know in the area is Clara's niece."

"Yeah, Brittany Stephens." He started to flicker like an old television signal.

"Why were you going there?" Clara would have a

conniption if she knew her niece, a newly divorced mother of two, had been hanging out with Wayne. "You're flickering. Why?"

"Brittany's none of your business. She wouldn't have done it," he said, words sharp and hard. He glanced down at his hands. "It takes a lot of energy to become visible. I'm feeling like I'm about to get my plug pulled. Thanks for helping me."

When he glanced back up Mina could've sworn there was genuine gratefulness in his eyes. The sudden shift from sullen, obnoxious jerk left Mina a little disoriented. "You're welcome." He couldn't leave yet. "Wait—if Brittany didn't do it, I don't have the faintest idea where to start."

"There I *can* help. I'm pretty sure you'll find my body in your shed." He dissolved with a crack of laughter.

EIGHT

"Yoo, hoo! Mina!" Nosey Turner called across the square.

Good gravy. Not Melissa again. Does she lay in wait to ambush people? Mina picked up her pace, zipping around the corner from the Police Department toward the Cup. Two hours of questioning left her little patience for the town gossip. She shoved the diner's glass door open. It narrowly missed the back of a large, plaid-shirted man who'd squeezed in with the other waiting customers.

She 'pardoned' her way through the twenty or so, then eyed the packed diner. Kayla, Rageena and Geri moved with economy through the tables carrying plates laden with food or tubs full of dirty dishes. When people noticed Mina, they stopped talking, until the whole place had grown eerily silent. Having all eyes focused on her made her skin crawl.

"Mina," Lois Dearborn, the Fellowship Church secretary, touched her shoulder. "I can't believe they found Wayne Beedy in your shed." Her poor attempt at a whisper had to have carried across the entire diner.

Mina barely suppressed the eye roll. "Me either." Was that a passive-aggressive way of saying Mina was a murderer or just a ridiculously blatant invitation to gossip. Either way, not very nice of her. Lois was new to the community, only nine months since she moved with the church's new Pastor, Donald Davis, from their old congregation in Georgia. The dynamic preacher had caused quite a stir with his charismatic service, and the pews started to fill more each week until you had to get there early for a seat. If Mina listened to gossip, hard to avoid in a small town's only diner, she'd already half-believe Lois and the Pastor were having an affair. *If* Mina listened to gossip. Her family had been the subject of enough speculation and ridicule to last a lifetime. She put little credence in idle talk.

As Mina slipped her way through the small crowd, she checked the red-cased clock in the dining area. One o'clock. It appeared the town had shown up trying to get the latest juicy details. Who was she to deny them the opportunity to put money in her bank account? For the next hour and a half, Mina pitched in, filling drink orders, bussing tables, delivering meals, and dodging thinly-veiled questions posed by everyone from Lois to Pastor Davis, who came in later with his pretty, if timid, wife.

Two hours later, enough slack developed for her to retreat to her office. She fell back into her chair with a gusty sigh and rubbed her gritty eyes. Instead of some private time with her husband last night, they'd had to deal with Wayne's body, which had, indeed, been found in her shed. The Justice of the Peace showed up from Eastland, nearly fifty miles away. Around three in the morning, the JP finally released the county ambulance service to take Wayne's body for examination by a coroner, all the way in Fort Worth. Since Eastland County had called in the Rangers for Beedy's escape, State Troopers kept watch over the shed until their crime scene people could come in this morning to properly search for clues.

Mina opened the Cup today, arriving at five o'clock for the breakfast crowd. Two hours of sleep wouldn't have been enough, even if she *had* been able to shut her eyes. At least the news of Wayne's discovery hadn't gotten out by the time the small, loyal crew of breakfast regulars filtered in.

Cowhands, ranchers, some local business leaders, and the Morning Boys, OP with a shiny new silver pickup with its paper tags. She could do those orders in her sleep—their preference of eggs, bacon, grits, and homemade biscuits never changed.

The phone in her back pocket vibrated. She pulled it out and answered it without checking caller ID. "'Lo."

"They just got done, packed up and left." Garrett said. "Chief Ruiz told me they got done with *you* two hours ago. You're rapidly earning yourself some severe discipline, young lady." His humorous tone fell flat.

Her exhaustion level didn't allow for a matching attempt or even the ability to blush at his innuendo. "Yeah, we got slammed. Apparently, I'm the hot topic right now. I bet the hardware store business is ticking up and some people will be sad to see you're not there." Garrett had many more gracious social skills than she. "So, you and the Chief have been comparing notes?"

"No, he came over after they finished your interview. Said he let the Texas Rangers do it, mainly because he's known you since you were a baby and was close to your parents. He feels protective about you, you know. I think he sees you a little like a daughter."

Warmth grew in her heart. He'd been a friend of her parents', and as a trooper, ended up working the wreck that had killed them. After that, he'd often stopped by the house to see her Granma. But he never failed to talk to Mina, Sunny, and Lacey. And he never treated them as kids to be pitied either. He was a good man. "Did he say they found anything in the shed?"

"Not much, though they tried. They believe someone dumped Wayne's body, that he was killed elsewhere, probably the night he escaped."

Whew. Which means they didn't really believe she'd killed him. Plus, it matched Wayne's account. She wouldn't trust him to not lie to her, even about how, when, and where he'd been murdered. "I figured as much. The bloodstain on his t-shirt appeared to be bigger on the left side of his chest. When we saw him in the shed last night, he was laying on his right side. I'm not a detective, but I'd say it was a clue he'd been moved."

Garrett chuckled. "They found some areas where they thought Wayne's heels might've dragged through the yard. And a tire track from a truck in some dirt in the alley. That's about it for now—how'd the interview go?"

"Uncomfortable. But those Rangers had nothing on a Maureen Flannigan interrogation." She laughed a little at her joke to break her tension, but it soon returned. "I guess good? They asked if I threatened to kill him and I said I did, but only after he threatened me. Practically the whole town heard me say it. Point for me was if I'd have killed him, why would I stick him in my own shed then call the cops? They did ask about him coming into the Cup, and I told them I thought I saw him, but I was pretty sure it was stress. I think they believed me." She lowered her voice to a whisper. "Like I'd tell them I saw his ghost?" The two no-nonsense Rangers, in their starched, white shirts with their round, silver badges on the breast, would've calmly consigned her to the loony bin.

"Speaking of ghosts, have you seen him today?" Garrett had kept his words light, but concern seeped through.

"Nope." Thank goodness. Garrett wasn't thrilled Wayne wanted her to solve his murder. "I haven't even had a second to start looking into it."

"Huh. From the way you described it, he sounded like he'd be dogging your heels twenty-four-seven."

"He said it took a lot of energy to become..." She searched for the word. "Corporeal. Maybe he's sleeping in."

Garrett chuckled. "By the way, Dad's filling in for

me at the store while the crime scene people were here, so I'll get Jake. Don't go running off without me. I don't like the idea of you looking into a murder all by yourself." This time he didn't bother to hide the unease. It was one thing to see ghosts. Another to investigate a murder.

Anyone willing to kill another would probably do it again to avoid discovery. "Not looking to go anywhere right now. I'm swamped. Love you."

She gazed at her desk and the mound of paperwork demanding attention. Investigating would have to wait. She signed onto her computer and began her orders for the café. Finally, she clicked the 'sleep' icon then propped her forehead in her hand. What she wouldn't give for a good three-hour nap. But the sooner she got started with her 'investigation', the less likely Wayne was to get annoyed with the lack of progress and pop in during…an intimate moment. She shuddered. She wouldn't put it past him to do it, too. A huge yawn threatened to dislocate her jaw. Maybe she could catch twenty. She swung her sneakered feet up on her desk and leaned back in her chair. As she closed her eyes, the sounds of cafe faded into the background.

"You okay?"

Mina started hard enough to tumble backward, but caught herself in time with a small screech. She tried to regain control of her galloping heart. Her hand massaged her chest over her t-shirt.

"Sorry I startled you," Clara said.

"It's fine." Mina waved it off. She needed to talk to the cook anyway. Wayne may have told her where to find his body, but she hadn't gotten any clues from it. Since Clara had practically adopted Brittany when Clara's sister ran away from her marriage fifteen years ago, the cook had topped Mina's priority list. "What's going on?"

"I was hoping Jimmy could come in to finish up the afternoon and evening? I know I'm supposed to close, but..." Her hands, clasped around the handles of her purse, tightened until little color remained.

Strange. If Clara had one quality, it was her reliability. "Sure. Not like you to leave in the middle of your shift, everything okay?"

The older woman swayed side to side on her orthopedic shoes several times, a sign of her distress. "The school called. Brittany didn't pick up the kids. I've called her several times. It's not like her to not answer. I'm...worried." Her face paled to where it matched her bloodless hands.

If Brittany was messed up with Wayne... Should she tell Clara? Mina discarded the idea when she couldn't come up with a suitable way to explain how she knew the two had some sort of entanglement.

"Maybe she had car trouble and her phone died." Mina pasted an encouraging smile on her face and looked up to meet the fretting woman's frown. "I'm sure you'll find her soon."

Chief Ruiz appeared at Clara's shoulder. He worked the brim of his straw hat through his fingers for a moment before saying, "Is there somewhere we can talk, Clara? You'll need to sit down. I've got some bad news."

NINE

"She's *not* dead?" If Clara hadn't been sitting in a chair at the back of the nearly empty restaurant, she may have collapsed with relief.

Thank goodness. Mina sat next to her and she covered her cook's hand with her own on the table top and gave it a reassuring squeeze.

"The deputy said the seatbelt and airbags saved her life when her vehicle went through the guardrail," Daniel said. "The gorge wall took the impact and her SUV landed on a ledge, instead of the two-hundred-foot drop. Heck of a piece of luck. Makes you want to go to church on Sunday." He shook his head in wonder. "A couple of seconds prior and she'd have plunged into the gorge, a couple of seconds later, she'd have run off the road, probably killing herself hitting rocks and trees."

"Thank you, thank you, thank you," Clara muttered, eyes closed.

Daniel's hand covered Clara's free hand. "They airlifted her to John Peter Smith in Fort Worth for possible head and internal injuries. A head wound bled pretty bad, but the paramedics got there fast and they said they thought she'd pull through. I can't imagine if someone hadn't seen her go over and called 911. She might've been there for a while."

Clara's eyes roamed the restaurant unfocused, as if she didn't know where to start.

To see her normally capable cook at a loss tugged at Mina's heart. "I'll pick up Brittany's kids, unless their father can do it." Mina said. "She just moved back to town and they're at Dew Drop Elementary, right?"

Clara nodded slowly, "Their father can't see them right now. I'm their guardian, in lieu of Brittany."

Poor kids. Divorce sucked, but when parents couldn't let go gracefully it had to be awful. "They can stay with us. Do you need someone to drive you to Fort Worth? Garrett will do it, you know."

Clara sucked in a deep breath and let it out slowly. "No, no. I'll be fine." Clara scrubbed at her eyes with one hand. "Don't know quite what to think. And I don't want to put you and Garrett out."

"Don't even worry about it. Let me know if you want to stay overnight and we'll keep them."

"I have to open tomorrow morning."

"Nope, I got it. You said Jimmy can come in and close with Kayla?"

Clara nodded slowly. "I called earlier to make sure he was available."

"Then scoot." Mina made shooing motions with her hands. "Unless you want Garrett to take you?"

"No. No. I'll be okay." Clara rose, then dug her keys from her purse. "If I'm staying at the hospital, you'll want clothes for the kids for tomorrow. They're renting Doc Bannister's place. I'll text you the address in case you need it." She finished working a key off the ring and handed it to Mina.

"I know Doc's house. You're staying with Brittany. Get some clothes and move along. Brittany needs you. We've got plenty of room in the house." Mina leveled a mock serious face. "I said, scoot. That's an order."

Clara spun and took a step then stopped and turned back. "When JT said you were buying the Cup, I worried because I'd heard the rumors about Sweetie Flannigan. I want you to know I'm proud to work for you and proud to call you a friend."

Tears leaked from the corners of Mina's eyes. She

dashed at them with the back of her hand. "Would you get going? You're ruining my reputation." *Sarcasm, the refuge for emotional cowards. Ha ha. Like you'd tell them why you turned over a new leaf. What would she think of you then?*

Clara whirled and marched out, Mina and Daniel tracking her exit through the kitchen service door.

Mina sniffed and rubbed her nose. "I better get going and pick up those kids." She put her hands flat on the table to push back her chair.

"She's right, you know," Chief Ruiz said. "Most people only see what they want. You've been a hard woman for many years, and I don't quite know why. But I've noticed a change lately." His teeth flashed under the bushy salt-and-pepper mustache. "And it looks good on you."

Tears threatened again. Mina almost blurted out her secrets to the man who'd often been like a father to her after the death of her parents. Though he'd always humored Maureen, Lacey and Sunny, he'd been firmly in her camp, practical and a disbeliever of all things paranormal. What would she tell him? She could see ghosts? She now believed in the Flannigan Gift? Wayne Beedy wanted her to investigate his murder? Her tears sucked back into their ducts.

"Good gravy. What is it with everyone today? Be nice to one person and they think you're gonna be nice to everyone." *Coward.* She shoved her chair back and rose. "I've got some kids to pick up."

TEN

Clara had obviously called ahead to warn the school. Laura Horne, Mina's second-grade teacher way back when, now the school's principal, stood under the entrance's awning. Next to her were Kinley of the blonde hair and eyes far beyond her years, as well as a younger boy, also blond, whose name Clara may have mentioned, but Mina could not for the life of her remember.

She threw her truck in park at the curb and hopped out at precisely half past four. "Hi, Laura. Congratulations. I'm sure the whole town will love having you back." She suppressed the wince at her awkward, forced cheer. Especially when with adulthood had come use of first names to combine with their history. She and Laura were only fifteen years apart, but little Mina had been in Laura's very first class as a teacher. Lucky lady.

"Mina." Laura had always been cool toward her, but today, the principal's tone would've frozen hell. Somehow, it didn't figure she still held a grudge from when seven-year-old Mina called her Horrible Horne to her face and refused to apologize. Surely she'd gotten the superior attitude when she'd moved to the Fort Worth school district. "I told them their mother had been in a car accident and they were going to stay with you for the night." Laura's nose rose a bit higher. It couldn't be any more plain she believed it to be a stupid idea.

Nice. And what a way to put it in front of the kids, too. No time to figure out what'd gotten in Laura's bonnet. She stuck her hand out to Kinley. "Hi, my name's Mina Shaffer, and I'm a friend of your Aunt Clara. She asked if you could stay with us for a little while your mom gets better."

The girl gave her the once down and up rake with a glance, then tilted her nose up a bit, a lot like Horrible Horn. "I'm Kinley Majors." The girl nodded her head toward her brother. "That's Trace. You're Jake's mom, right?"

Mina dropped her hand. "Yep." Maybe the lack of manners was due to the stress of Brittany's accident and having to stay with unknown people. "We better get going so Miss Horne can go home." She turned to the scowling woman. *Laura could win a national championship in an RBF contest.* Had she learned the superior look in Fort Worth? Mina barely held her tongue on the thought—old habits died hard. Instead, she said, "I don't know how long we'll have them. I'm sure Clara will keep you up to date. Y'all ready to roll?" she asked Kinley and Trace with a smile.

They trooped to the truck, both hopping in the pickup's backseat and buckling up like pros. Trace really should've had a booster seat, but they'd taken Jake's out a couple of months ago. She'd have to root it out of the shed. Huh. Shed. Wonder where Wayne had hidden himself. She dismissed that thought, now was not the time to conjure him up.

Suppressing a shrug, she pulled out to the street, right this time, instead of left toward town. It should be a straight shot to the Bannister house in a couple of minutes. "Aunt Clara gave me a key so we can get you some clothes for tomorrow. Do y'all have homework?"

"Trace is too young for homework. He's only in first grade. I did mine while I waited for *you* to show up."

Mina glanced in her rearview mirror. A little snooty for seven. *Ha! What were* you *like back then?*

She should cut the kid a break. Kinley found out her mother had been in a bad car wreck, not to mention she was a focal point in a nasty divorce. Mina thanked her lucky stars she'd come to her senses and Jake didn't have to go through a mess like that.

A large black pickup truck, similar to the one OP Boyd replaced, came speeding in the other direction, a good twenty-five miles per hour more than the posted thirty-five. Good grief. So close to the school zone.

Kinley said, "That's Dad's truck."

Mina checked her rearview mirror. "How do you know it's your daddy's?" West Texas had its fair share of big, black pickups.

"It had a 'Majors Construction' sign on his door." By the girl's tone, she must've executed an eye roll a teen would envy.

"Maybe he came by to see if you guys were there after school." Even though he wasn't supposed to be seeing them at all according to Clara.

"He's not supposed to see us right now," Kinley said. "The judge said so." It sounded rather parroted from an adult conversation and Mina's heart went out to the Major's children.

"He yells and makes momma cry." Those were the first words Mina had heard Trace utter this whole time. Maybe big sis said enough for the both of

GHOSTS, PIES, & ALIBIS   65

them. Or maybe their daddy discouraged conversation.

"Sometimes grownups hurt each other." The platitude grated on her nerves, but what else could be said? Apparently nothing, because she got no reaction.

Soon enough, she pulled down the driveway to the big fifties ranch occupied until three years ago by Doc Bannister. The bushes needed trimming along with the grass, which was mostly weeds now. It's a shame how people treated rentals. But then a single mother with youngsters might deserve a break on yard maintenance. Lord knew it was all she and Garrett could do to keep up the rambling Victorian she inherited from Granma, let alone the yard, which took up two city lots.

She continued down the driveway lined with enormous tufts of pampas grass to the carport which had its own side entrance. As she rolled under the shade, she took in the screen door. It hung open. Behind it, the door seemed ajar. She stared at it from the inside of the truck, nibbling on her lower lip.

Did Brittany forget to shut it?

Hard to imagine anyone leaving a door open on a blazing August day like today. Foreboding thrilled through her. She shook it off. This was Dew Drop, over one hundred miles from the big city of Fort

Worth. Most everyone knew everyone else. No one would've burglarized the house.

Yet... She scanned the front yard again. Overgrown hedges at the front of the property screened the house from the street. A line of mature oaks hid it from the nearest neighbor. It would be a good bet if someone had broken in, no one would've seen it. Still, this was Dew Drop. To be safe, she told the children, "Stay here 'til I get back." She hopped out.

Creepy tingling broke out across the back of her neck, raising the fine hairs under her ponytail. She glanced around. Wayne? Despite her glances over her shoulder, no ghosts—or people for that matter—appeared. A deep breath, a wince, then she pulled the rusted metal-framed screen door open further, yet it didn't make a sound. Or it could be she couldn't hear the squeak over the thundering of her heart. *Stop. You should call Garrett.* Her feet took the two steps to the door, not heeding her sensible side.

She stuck her head through the opening and peeped in. "Hello?"

No answer. No rustling. She'd always had a weird ability to sense if someone was around, as if they gave off an electrical wavelength she could hear. No one was in the house that she could tell by the frequency in the buzzing in her ears. She stepped inside.

The door led to a living area. Heavy drapery intended to keep out the brutal summer sun hung in tatters. Her once racing heart came to a screeching halt. She pushed a ruined curtain panel wider to allow more light so she could gauge the destruction.

Cuss words had been scrawled on every wall in traffic-cone orange spray paint, most started with the letter 'b', some with 'c'. The couch had been turned over, all the of the cushions and pillows shredded. Pictures and other small items swept from shelves, broken. A small wooden sign, 'Children are the Heart of Our Family' lay on the floor near her feet, snapped in two. There hadn't been a square inch which the vandal hadn't touched in the family room. In the adjoining eating area, a chair still hung from the wall where it had been thrown and stuck in the drywall. The remaining seating had been beaten to matchsticks. More nasty graffiti marred these walls as well. Her mouth went dry. *The kids can't see this.*

This time, her feet listened to her sensible side and retreated to the carport. Once past the screen door, she pulled out her phone.

Instead of Garrett, she called Daniel Ruiz.

ELEVEN

The unforgiving late summer sun slanted its burning tentacles onto the concrete footprint of Doc Bannister's carport.

"Seems to be a right bit of trouble around you lately." The Chief pulled his straw hat from his head a wiped his brow.

Too much trouble. Wayne's murder and now this? Could it be somehow part of Wayne's death? He'd said he was headed to her house. Without a shred of proof, or the ability to tell Daniel where she got the information, she kept her trap shut.

Luckily, the house stood near Dew Drop's limits. Only about one hundred yards further north and it would've fallen into the county's jurisdiction. She would've had to deal with an unknown when it came to Eastland County Sheriff's Office. Dew Drop sat at the farthest east arm of the county, ten miles south of Interstate 20 off State Highway 16. Long ago, the tiny city's residents determined they needed their own police, not a sheriff's department outpost. They'd more than earned their money today. Chief Ruiz had stayed at the house until they'd removed Wayne's body early this morning, had been at the station when she showed at ten for her interview with the Rangers, now her phone said five fifteen in the afternoon. A murder investigation and a burglary in this small town within two days and only eight officers for the department?

Should she tell him what the girl saw? The possibility of the dad being dangerous meant the truth won out. "Hey, uh, as we were driving here from the elementary, Kinley said her dad's truck passed us going the opposite direction. Big black truck, oversized tires, 'Majors Construction' sign on the door."

"Interesting." Daniel rubbed his chin with the crook of his index finger.

"That was according to Kinley. I saw the truck after it passed. Pretty sure it was a Ford, but don't quote me on it. Saw a white square on the driver's door, but other than that, it looked a lot like about half the trucks around here. Extended cab, big tires, full-sized bed. Like OPs, but maybe a year or two older." She followed Daniel's gaze over her shoulder and found Kinley staring at them through the light tint on her pickup windows. "Do you have to talk to her tonight? She's had a rough day."

The corners of his mouth dropped. "I can't anyway. By law she has to have a parent or guardian if I question her. I can use what you said and follow up with her mother."

Mina's shoulder's drooped. "Another statement?" She just wanted to go home and crawl in bed.

"Not for this. I can use hearsay if I have to at this point. If Brittany won't let me talk to her, and we need it, I'll get one from you. Besides, I might be able to review the camera footage from the school."

"From the school?"

"They put a new system in over the summer with some state grant money for protection. They cover every square inch of the campus, plus the road in front. If he went past you in the direction, I bet they captured him. Ah, here's D-P-S crime scene."

A black SUV had come to a stop next to Daniel's police car. A tall, thin woman exited the driver's side, her steel gray hair pulled back into an efficient bun at her neck. A much shorter and rounder man exited the passenger side. Both wore black polo shirts, black army pants and combat boots. The woman sketched a wave. The two turned to the back of their vehicle.

Mina's attention pivoted back to the Chief.

"Why are they here? I thought you guys would search the scene." *Exactly who's been watching too many true-crime shows?*

"They were still in town putting together their evidence from your shed. I asked them to come. The scene's large, and they're way more efficient than we are."

She stifled a huge yawn. "Umm. Hey, it's getting late. Can I go? I'll have to stop by Walmart for some clothing for the children, get them fed, then to bed." *Then I get to go to bed.*

"We've got your elimination prints from earlier. You only touched the handle and the door where you showed me, right?"

"Nowhere else. I can pinky-swear if you need me to. I draw the line at blood, though."

He laughed. "Now there's the Mina I remember."

She sobered. "Would you let me know if you talk to Brittany's husband? If he did this..." Mina had her own family to worry about and whoever trashed this house could do a number on her own home or the Cup.

"I'll keep your name out of it if I can, but I'll let you know if I talk to him."

"Thanks." She climbed back into her pickup.

"Why are we leaving?" Kinley asked. "I want to get my clothes." The whine on the last sentence set

Mina's nerves on edge. Daniel hadn't been the only one going on short-sleep today.

"I told you. Because someone broke into your house." Mina used her backup camera and mirrors to maneuver around the law enforcement cars. "The Chief said they probably won't be done until late." She backed into the grass then continued forward down the driveway. "We'll go to Walmart to get some pj's, and a set of clothing for you both for tomorrow."

"Walmart? We don't buy clothes from there."

Snoo-tee. Mina kept straight, since they traveled in the direction to both the store and the house. She'd gotten her own jeans shorts from the retailer, as well as most of her wardrobe. She either shopped there, or Olivia's Cowboy Chic Boutique, which carried adult clothing too 'fancy' for the Cup where she spent most of her waking hours. She flashed her best Sweetie Flannigan fake smile at the child. "Sure. You can sleep in the clothes you have and wear them to school tomorrow."

They continued for a moment until Kinley said, "I don't want to wear these clothes tomorrow." Sass had disappeared from the child's words.

"Walmart it is."

On the way, she called to advise Garrett of her whereabouts and ETA. She'd called him earlier after getting ahold of Daniel. The idea he worried about her caused a warmth in her belly. She'd been operating on her own within her marriage for so long.

She'd expected a struggle at Walmart, but in short order, they found everything necessary, and checked out without a major hit to the bank account. On to the house for food and bed.

"You live *here?*"

For once the child didn't sound as if she was grudgingly slumming it. "Yep."

The huge Victorian never failed to impress Mina. The gingerbread details, shingling, and daring maroon-forest green-mustard color scheme made it stand out on a block of beautiful and once-beautiful early 1900s homes. She and Garrett ensured they kept it in immaculate shape. If his parents hadn't sold the family hardware store to him with generous terms, she doubted they'd have been able to afford the old home's costly upkeep. Quite a difference from the seventies ranch house Brittany had rented.

Mina stopped before she got to the porte-cocher where Garrett waited for them. The overhang and its supporting columns had been built not long after the turn of the century. They wouldn't be able to open the pickup's doors if she'd pulled through, even if they hadn't turned the shaded area into a terrace. Garrett had risen from his seat in one of the adirondack chairs and approached the truck. Jake raced from around the corner from the backyard. "Mom, I saw—" He skidded to a halt.

Mina followed his open-mouthed stare to Kinley, who had climbed down and stood staring up at their house with fascination. Ah, puppy love.

Garret took the bags Mina had in her hand into one of his, then wrapped his arms around her, his chin resting on her head. She relaxed into his embrace and, for a moment, allowed herself to acknowledge her exhaustion.

"Jake needs to talk to you," he murmured. "Alone." He released her and turned with his signature kid-winning grin. "You must be Kinley and you're Trace?" The driveway's decomposed granite crunched under his boots as he led the kids the short distance to the side door.

"Hi, Jake." Kinley shot a look from under her lashes.

It appeared Jake would stand there, jaw gaping, but he rallied. "Hi, Kinley."

Mina stifled the desire to roll her eyes and headed her son's way. That city girl was way too advanced for Dew Drop's country boys. "Come on, kiddo. We can talk in the gazebo."

TWELVE

Mina and Jake crossed through the grass, shaded by the hundred-year old live oaks planted by Flannigan ancestors. The hot, brisk Texas summer breeze rustled through their leaves and slid across her nape under her ponytail, bringing the tiniest bit of relief from the late summer temperature. She resisted the temptation to take Jake's hand. He'd started pushing back on all the 'baby' things she did, like kiss him goodbye in the carpool line. With Kinley possibly looking out the window, she didn't want to embarrass him.

He sat next to her in the ornate domed structure set in the far side of the yard. The Pinkerton's one-story Queen Ann Victorian peeked through the screen of crepe myrtles. Jake's feet still didn't completely reach the floor, and the toes of his sneakers stubbed the painted wood. They sat for a couple of minutes in silence. She slid a glance to his bowed head, brown hair glinting with copper highlights he'd gotten from his father. Though a quiet child, usually he'd get to the point faster than this.

Please tell me this has nothing to do with Kinley. "Things okay in school? Second grade going okay?" she prompted instead.

"Uh huh."

She could barely make out his profile. So serious. "What's up, then? Wait. Let me guess." She kept her tone light. "You've decided second grade isn't for you and you're going to run away and join the circus."

"No."

Did she detect a hint of humor? "Then it must be you've decided to take up professional bowling."

A huff of laughter, then, "No."

"I know." She smacked her forehead with her palm. "It's obvious. You've decided to take up ostrich herding."

"No, mom." Genuine laughter this time with an eye roll.

"Then I'm out of guesses. You'll have to tell me."

"That man came to see me."

She stilled and went to full alert. "What man?"

"The ghost."

"Wayne Beedy? The ghost from yesterday?" An

icy fury threatened to overtake her, but she shoved it aside for later. "What did he say?"

Jake lifted his eyes to her. "He wrote 'mom hurry'."

"Wrote?"

"In the dirt at school. It's how they talk to me."

"They don't speak to you?"

He shook his head side to side. "Only write."

Wow. She'd assumed if she could talk to Beedy, Jake could as well. What other differences were there? "We haven't gotten time to talk about this. When did you first start seeing them?"

"I don't know. They've always been there." He shrugged his thin shoulders.

Like her. Until she tuned them out. "How did you know they weren't real people?"

He stared off toward the neighbor's house. "I asked Granma once why the man I saw in dad's store had a glow around him. She said she didn't see anyone."

Huh. Another difference. "Do they always glow for you?"

"Only when there isn't any light. It's not really bright."

In its turn of the century building, Shaffer's hardware wasn't the best lit store. "Do they ever...

scare you?" She never remembered seeing a scary one.

"There was one once. Granma showed me how to protect myself and she schmuh-schmuged the house."

"Smudged?"

"Yeah. Now Lacey does it when she comes home."

Mina had asked Lacey to stop the practice after Granma died, but her younger sister refused. Mina had been angry about it, but what could she do? Ban Lacey from the house? Yet all she'd been doing was keeping Mina's son safe. Her stomach sank. Mina hadn't been there for him. For when he saw his first ghost, or when he'd seen a bad one. Not until now. "How often does she do it? I need to start." She should. Her stubborn refusal to acknowledge the Flannigan Gift meant she wasn't protecting Jake. Her *son*. It would end now. And maybe it would keep Wayne out as well.

"Once a week. If Lacey can't do it, sometimes they come in the house."

Like Wayne last night. *Good gravy.* It'd been three weeks since Lacey went back to college. Is that why Wayne had been able to get inside? "Have you seen any ghosts in there lately?"

He stared at his sneakers. "Nope."

Thank goodness. "You said there was something else Granma taught you to do?"

He nodded. "Yeah. It's hard at first. She said I had to put up a wall in my mind. They can't come through, bad or good."

A little like she had done to not see them at all? "It's hard, huh?"

"Granma said you're really good at it, and that's why you don't see them anymore. I can make them go away, but they come back after a while, sometimes."

Whoa. She'd done it naturally for almost her whole life. "The bad ones?"

"All of them."

She slapped at mosquito on her arm. Interesting he had to sacrifice the gift completely to get rid of the bad ghosts. Would that mean she would, too? "Do you see bad ones all the time?"

"No. Hardly ever. And they usually go away when I put up the wall."

"What do the bad ones look like?" She'd only seen Wayne. Shades poked at her memory, but nothing she could remember led to a reaction to bad ghosts, just the living teasing her for seeing them at all.

A shudder wracked his body. "You'll know," he whispered.

Goosebumps marched across her skin. She looked over her shoulders, searched the deep shadows of the yard. Nothing evil seemed to lurk. Probably only her imagination. *Okay. Time to lighten the mood.* She punched his shoulder lightly. "Enough about the ghosts. So, this was all about Wayne Beedy, huh."

"No. I got a B on my math quiz." He looked up at her through his long, curly lashes.

Sneaky boy. "Did you ask Ms. Chilcote what you did wrong?"

"Yes ma'am."

"And you understand it now?"

He nodded his head.

"You know we don't get mad if you don't get an 'A'. Only if you don't try and you don't try to learn why. You were trying right?" At the jerk of his chin, she continued. "You can always ask me or dad. We'll be happy to help."

The smile she loved appeared, now with two of his upper incisors missing. "Thanks mom."

"You're welcome, kiddo." She spied his hands, streaked with dirt from playing. "Head on inside and wash up for dinner. Tell Kinley and Trace, too. I'll be there in a minute."

He threw his arms around her, an unexpected gift of the younger boy usually eschewed by older

Jake. "I love you, Mom. I'm glad you see them now, too." He raced off across the grass on his coltish legs then disappeared around the back of the house.

She stared at the crepe myrtles at their property line, not really seeing the Pinkerton's house behind the lacy fronds. So much to learn. How in the world had she been that blind? If she'd been honest with herself she'd have known all Jake revealed, how to protect herself, how to protect him.

Shame, thick and bitter clogged her throat. Mina lifted her eyes to the mustard-colored dome above her. "I'll do better, Granma. I promise." *You can't see the road ahead if you're looking behind you,* whispered through her mind. Another of Granma's sayings. She'd had a load of them, one for every occasion. It certainly fit. And, more importantly, it felt right. A...sign.

Now you believe in signs? Mina snorted a half-laugh. She saw ghosts.

Why not believe in signs?

THIRTEEN

The next afternoon, Mina pushed the heavy door open and entered *Cowboy Chic Boutique.* She wanted to get something new and nice. Something that would make Garrett's eyes glow with appreciation. And other than Walmart or driving to Fort Worth, which Mina had no time to do, Olivia's store was her answer. Plus, her friend usually gave her a little discount, something which Mina reciprocated with pie.

"Girl, you haven't stopped by for a visit in a month of Sundays! Where have you been hiding yourself?" Olivia sashayed around the corner of her barn wood-clad cash register stand. Bangles tinkled, layered necklaces swayed. Colorful embroidery covered her denim-colored tank, and sleek, white crop pants over nude, strappy sandals completed her look. If anyone could be the opposite to Mina's pragmatic dress style—jeans, t-shirt, and sneakers—it'd be Olivia Sutton and her boho-cowgirl style. She brushed her long ash-blonde hair over her shoulder. Danged if it didn't still have luscious curls at half-past two in the afternoon. Mina's dark auburn hair would've been a frizzy mess by now if not pulled back into a ponytail. Mentally, Mina shrugged. Looking great had to be a hazard of working in a retail store versus running around in a restaurant.

Mina braced and, true to form, her friend squeezed the life out of her. Olivia did everything over the top. How the angry little girl and the girl who lived her life out loud had come to be life-long friends still boggled Mina's mind.

"Where else *have* I been? At the Cup. But I haven't seen you there either." Mina fished for her friend's sudden disappearance from the diner.

Olivia's cheeks grew rosier under the artfully-applied blush. "I, uh..." Her tanned shoulders slumped. "Okay. I'm dieting. Thirty stinks. And I have absolutely no willpower where your pies are concerned."

Mina's eyes flicked down to her friend's trim figure. "Good gravy. Like you need to diet. I was beginning to worry you didn't like me anymore."

"How could you think—oh, you're joking." She

laughed, rich and musical. "How could I not like you?"

Mina lifted an eyebrow. "You know me. I rub people the wrong way sometimes."

"They don't know the real you. You here for a chat?" Olivia swung her arm toward two overstuffed brown leather chairs near the dressing rooms halfway down the side wall where weary men often waited for their wives.

"I'd love to, but I've had to give Clara a bit of time to tend to Brittany, and I'm running breakfast and half of lunch. I'm behind on my office work and I need to get Jake, Kinley and Trace in an hour."

Olivia's mouth twisted. "Ugh. The joys of small business ownership. Once the Iced Tea Festival is over, I'm happy for a little break."

"If Wayne Beedy hadn't ruined the festival's receipts on Saturday, I might've been able to bring on Jimmy full time, but I need to keep my head above water if I'm to stay on plan. But, I want to get something for the picnic." Mina clung stubbornly to her five-year plan to pay off the Cup. Except for this month. Even if she could write off the surveillance system she and Garrett planned to install this weekend, it still came out of the Cup's pocket.

Olivia's blue eyes sparkled. "Oh, little lady, have I got something for you." She grabbed Mina's arm and tugged her toward the back. She held up a cobalt-blue sundress with bright embroidery along the hem and its elasticized neckline. "It's a tunic—a little long for most, but too short for people to wear as a dress. Except for a petite lady like you. *And* it's in an extra small *and* on sale." With a happy curl of her light coral glossed lips, she whisked the not-a-sundress over her shoulder and added a skirt and a top. Then some crop pants and more pieces until she started to hunch a little to carry the load.

Mina held up a hand. "Hold on. I only have a couple of minutes before I need to get back. You have more than enough for me right now." She shuddered at the thought of trying on all of outfits.

Olivia swept the curtain aside from one of the fitting rooms and began to load the waiting hooks. "Only try on what you want. I know how allergic to clothes shopping you are."

Mina tossed her a grateful smile. "Thanks. And I know how much you love making people look good, so I'll do my best." She slid the drape across the rod and reached for the not-a-sundress first since it had spoken to her most. Its button-down style might give her a shirtwaist look, a term she'd learned from Olivia over the years. She tugged the shoulders down a bit, but something didn't work. She turned both ways to look at herself in the mirror, but no matter the angle, she still looked like a blue rectangle. Story of her life. Short and built like a boy.

"Well?"

Mina pushed aside the curtain. "I think it's a no."

"Wait. It had a belt." Olivia hustled to the sale rack and came right back. "Here." She wrapped the wide strip of matching blue fabric around Mina's nonexistent waist and knotted it with an artful loop, then bloused the top just so and tugged the sleeves until it reached the outermost of Mina's shoulders. "Now." She put her hands on Mina's upper arms and urged her to rotate to the mirror.

Mina caught her breath. Even above her white tennis shoes, the not-a-sundress flattered her creamy skin, made her green-blue eyes flash. It stopped an inch above her knee and not quite off-the-shoulder, acceptable for church, too. Sometimes it paid to be petite.

"Don't worry about the other outfits. This is it." A self-satisfied grin crossed Olivia's face. "I knew it would be."

Mina stuffed her hands on her hips. "Then why pull all the other stuff? You trying to scare me?"

"In case The Meanest Girl West of the Mississippi didn't like this." The way Olivia said it, with warm humor, took the sting from Mina's other nickname.

"Ha! Very funny." She whipped the curtain closed as the front bell rang indicating Olivia had customers.

For fun, she flipped through the remaining clothing. A denim skirt and white eyelet top caught her eye. *Why not.* She probably wouldn't like it better anyway. She unknotted the belt.

"Hi, Olivia." Nosey Turner's voice carried across the shop and through the fabric hiding Mina in the dressing room. "We're here to find something for the picnic."

Good gravy. Maybe she could pay Olivia later and sneak out the back door so she wouldn't have to deal with the gossipy woman.

"Anything in particular you're looking for?" Olivia's cheer rang true. Mina wished she could manage the same.

"No, we'll browse, thanks," Melissa said.

Mina pulled the dress over her head and smoothed her hair down. Good thing she'd decided to try on another outfit and was hidden in the dressing room. Nosey would want all the juicy details of Wayne being found in Mina's shed. *Gah. What a menace.*

Hushed voiced murmured along in conversation until they drifted near the dressing rooms.

"I know," Nosey hissed. "I can't get her aside to tell me anything."

"Why not? She knows the police chief, right? The body was found on her property, so she should know."

Mina couldn't figure out who was with Nosey. The low voice tickled along her memory, but it didn't call to mind anyone.

"I bet she's doing it out of spite. You know she's The Meanest Girl West of the Mississippi." They both laughed.

Somehow when Olivia or Garret said it, Mina didn't mind. Not so much now.

"I don't know, Melissa." The unknown woman said. "Didn't you tell me she's gotten nicer after she and Garrett reconciled?"

Mina had to strain to hear what the woman said, then caught herself eavesdropping. Her cheeks flushed with fiery heat. Goodness. She was no better than Nosey herself.

"I bet he had to tell her he was gone for good unless she straightened up and flew right." Nosey's self-righteous tone set Mina's teeth on edge. "Don't know why he took her back anyway. Stacey Boyd salivated for their divorce. Word is she went to the Shaffer ranch and prop-o-sitioned Garrett."

"Melissa!" The woman's scandalized whisper said, *Tell me more*.

Fury blew through Mina, evaporating any remaining shame at the eavesdropping. Stacey had ten years on Garrett. The darned woman needed to find someone else's man to prove she still had her former beauty queen looks. Mina almost pulled the curtain aside, then caught sight of the blue dress clutched in her hand. In her plain white bikini panties and bra, she'd give Nosey something to talk about. She dropped her hand and began yanking on her shorts. Those women were going to get a piece of her mind.

"Yep. You remember the cold snap we had in March? Stacey went out there with nothing on but her mink coat and what God gave her." Nosey tittered.

Who does that anymore? Mina pulled her Tea Cup t-shirt over her head and didn't bother with smoothing her hair toward its ponytail. She was going to give the woman the blistering she deserved. She reached for the curtain.

"That's not all Stacey's been up to," the woman said. "I heard she had been seeing Wayne Beedy."

FOURTEEN

Mina gasped, then covered her mouth with her hand. Stacey Boyd? The woman married to that overbearing OP?

"Did you hear something?" Nosey's voice rose.

Mina could picture Melissa looking over her shoulder to see if anyone had overheard her gossip. The long curtain should hide Mina's legs, but just in case, she put one foot up on the wooden seat, then the other until she perched on the wood-clad square like a ridiculous little bird.

"I didn't hear anything," the unidentified woman said. "You know these old buildings creek and moan. Besides Olivia's on the other side of the shop."

Please go back to Beedy and Stacey. Please go back to Beedy and Stacey. Mina had so little time lately, this could be another lead.

Like a dog with a bone, Nosey couldn't let something that juicy go. "How did you hear she was seeing Wayne?"

A pause. "I didn't really *hear* it. I saw her and Wayne in her car."

Mina managed to contain her gasp this time, but Nosey couldn't.

"You okay?" Olivia called from across the shop.

"Fine, fine," Nosey called out, obviously impatient to be back to the tidbit. A small squeak said someone was making a pretense at looking for the picnic outfit. "You said they were in her car?"

"I was so shocked I couldn't help but watch," the woman said in a stage whisper. She had to be right outside the curtain. "But then, they started shouting at each other. She pulled a gun on him from her purse and told him to get out. He did and was using the most foul language after she drove off."

"Oh, my stars. I'm going to have to sit on that one." A *plop* sounded as Nosey's generous rear hit the leather of a chair on the other side of the wall from Mina.

She could understand Melissa's need. Wayne and Stacey? Maybe in a relationship?

Leather crinkled as if the other chair gained an occupant. "And that's not all of it. As he got out she said she'd *kill* him."

"No." Nosey probably clutched the pearls she wore every day. Her grandmother gave them to her for high school graduation twenty years ago and Mina doubted she took them off, even for bed.

"Yes. Kill him. Then he yelled she'd be sorry." The cat that ate the cream couldn't have sounded more satisfied.

Holy herd of longhorns. Had Wayne's murder just been solved?

"Where were you?" Melissa whispered

"In the Dairy Bar parking lot. She tore off in her Mercedes. I was afraid he would see me, but he walked off."

"When did this happen?"

"Just before the Iced Tea Festival."

Melissa chuckled, evil and low. "Wouldn't the Chief love to know about *that*."

The woman gasped. "You think she killed Wayne?"

"Mina, are you doing okay in there?" Olivia called, singsong, from across the store.

Dang it. Mina hopped down from her perch. Her friend's kindness couldn't have come at a worse time. Though Mina wanted to stomp on the two women for gossiping about her and Garrett, she'd have to brave it out for the sake of Beedy's murder. Instead, she whipped open the curtain, the blue not-a-sundress on its hanger in her hand. "I think this is it, Olivia." Mina stopped, almost running into Lois Bonney, the church secretary. Ah, the voice she didn't recognize. She needed to go to church more often.

"Mina." Nosey's snobbish tone dragged Mina's attention from Lois.

"Hey, there, Melissa." She flashed a bright smile toward the awful woman. "I didn't know you two were friends."

"Just doing a bit of shopping." Lois's face had achieved a bright shade of red. As it should. The comments about Mina and Garrett deserved some serious penance. Nosey had lost that shame long ago.

"I heard we're in for a treat from Pastor Davis this week. I believe Proverbs 10:18 will be the focus of his sermon." Mina wasn't much for Bible passages, but with all the crappy stuff people had attributed to her family, she sure knew the passages regarding gossip.

If possible, Lois's cheeks stained a deeper crimson.

"Proverbs 10:18?" Nosey's brows climbed her forehead. "What's it say?"

"Never mind." Lois waived Melissa off, a mild sneer on her lips. She directed her next comment to Mina. "I hope to see you in church then."

Touché. Mina and Garrett's attendance would never be called stellar. "Sure will." Mina twitched the blue not-a-sundress on its hanger. "Wanted to make sure I had something suitable for the picnic, after all, we want to make sure we raise enough money to get those kids on their mission trip." She followed her comment with a saccharine smile, then flounced off toward Olivia who had been surveying the exchange with avid curiosity.

"See you, Olivia." Nosey pulled Lois along toward the heavy oak door with its large inset window.

"Sure." Olivia's careless reply from behind the register indicated she didn't care a bit if either darkened her door again. She tracked their progress until the heavy door shut behind them. "What was that about?"

"Gossip." The need to confide in her best friend beat at her. "It seems Stacey Boyd showed up at Shaffer Ranch when Garrett and I were separated and propositioned him." Mina's heart sunk. Though forty-something, more than a decade older than Mina, Stacey still had the height, the gorgeous blonde hair, the face, and the figure. All the things Mina didn't have.

"He's smart enough to run away from that hot

mess," Olivia said, her words drier than the Monahans Sand Dunes.

Mina's head knew it, but her heart couldn't help but hurt. "But it ticks me off Stacey thought he was free game."

"Stacey thinks *all* men are free game." Olivia's mouth twisted.

The bitterness of the words caught Mina's attention. "What?"

Olivia huffed an aggrieved breath. "During the Tea Festival's Library Auction, she came on to Waylon. 'No' wasn't in her vocabulary. I had to help her understand." Olivia and her husband Waylon, named after the one and only country singer, were as devoted a couple as Mina had ever seen.

Mina's mouth hung open and she shut it with a snap. "Why didn't you tell me?"

"You were busy with the aftermath of Wayne at the Cup, and we've barely had time to get together to really talk. The mouth on that drunk woman would make a sailor blush." She shook her head with arch disapproval.

Stacey owned an antiques shop two doors down from the Cowboy Chic Boutique. Mina could only imagine how the proximity grated on Olivia.

Mina needed a second opinion. Nosey's penchant for gossip was well known and she never seemed to care if it was true or not. Even if the information had come from Lois, Mina had to put it in the same box. "What would you say if Stacey was seen in a car with Wayne Beedy?"

"Ewww." Olivia's nose wrinkled with the word and a visible shudder rippled through her. "I'd say she'd lost her danged mind. What would she have in common with Wayne?"

"I don't know." Mina couldn't help the impulse to look over her shoulder, *a la* Nosey Turner when she had a particularly sweet piece of information, then related the conversation she'd overheard. Guilt roiled, but she needed a neutral perspective. Gossip or a real possibility?

Olivia rested her chin in her hand as she listened. "Wow. I bet the police would love to have those details. Totally a motive for his murder. Or at least a place to start."

Mina couldn't help trying to poke holes in the idea she should notify Chief Ruiz. "But without knowing the reason why, is it really a motive? I mean, I know you probably never have, but I've told someone I'd kill them before. I wouldn't have, but if they'd ended up dead, I'm pretty sure I'd be a suspect. Like with Wayne."

"But have you pulled a gun on someone or

screamed it at the top of your lungs?" Olivia canted her head to the side with a lift to her brow.

"No." The more they discussed it, the more it seemed Stacey had a reason to be on the list of suspects in Wayne Beedy's murder. It might solve the case. Then a vindictive spark lit. She could report the information in return for coming on to Garrett and Waylon. Stacey's husband, OP, had a jealous streak as hot as a Texas midsummer's day. As quickly as it came, the urge for revenge fizzled. The new Mina couldn't do it to another person. Old Mina might not have been so nice. "She could have a totally legit alibi."

"Sure." Olivia snorted a laugh. "And cattle can fly."

Mina traced the pattern in the countertop's faux wood grain with her fingertip. "I could see if she has an alibi. That way it's not just gossip."

Olivia's eyes narrowed on her friend. "I'm kind of surprised you listened to Melissa and Lois. You're not usually into the gab."

"I was annoyed about them gossiping about me and Garrett, then they started talking about Wayne and Stacey, and it seems they have information they aren't giving to the cops." She should report it. No. "Imagine the blowback if it turns out she had an alibi and they found out it was me who told the police?"

"Why do you care? Wouldn't it be best if the Chief figures that out? Besides, it's Wayne."

How could she not tell her best friend she saw ghosts? That she'd been wrong about the Flannigan Gift this whole time? Her eyes strayed to the oversized clock behind Olivia. Five minutes to three. Dang it. She'd have to hurry. "It just doesn't seem right to accuse someone based on gossip. But still, people shouldn't hide stuff or the wrong person goes to jail. Worse, the right person goes free."

She'd tell Olivia about the ghosts soon. Right now, she had an antiques dealer to go see.

FIFTEEN

Mina paused, hand on the enormous oak door's handle. On its inset glass, *Boyd's Fine Antiques* had been traced in tasteful gold paint, and an elegant cardboard placard announced the shop *Open*. A small, equally tasteful sign with the store's name sat above on the brick, in stark contrast to the *Antiques Barn* sign across the square which had been executed in twenty-five foot, glaring neon.

Still wondering why she agreed to help the awful man despite his threats, Mina pushed open the heavy panel.

Stacey sat at a delicate desk mid-way down the length of the store, focused on a laptop. She lifted her head, a welcoming beauty-queen smile on her face at the ring of the shop's brass bell. It faded once she saw who had entered.

"Mina." She closed the lid of the computer with a decided click and adjusted her lips to the wattage of bare tolerance. She raked cool blue eyes down as Mina moved toward the desk. "What can I do for *you* today?"

Ohh... First the visual inspection suggesting Mina lacked in the appearance department, then the tone saying Mina couldn't afford anything in Boyd's Fine Antiques. The combo made her want to smack the woman, considering what she'd just learned from Nosey and Lois. She tamped down her anger with a vicious stomp and pasted on a bogus smile.

"Not much. I was down at Olivia's." Mina held up her bag. "I ran into Nos—Melissa Turner and Lois Bonney. They said they'd forgotten to ask you for a church picnic auction item, but they were running late to a meeting and didn't have time to come and ask you in person. I said I had a moment, so, here I am." She forced her most cheerful voice, as if she didn't have the right to rip every one of those perfectly set blonde beauty-queen curls from Stacey's head. *Down, girl.*

The faintest of frowns tugged at Stacey's brow and she rose from her chair. "I dropped off the donation last week."

Uh oh. Mina had banked on the idea Stacey didn't have anything in the shop which could be donated. The items for sale weren't crammed in every nook and cranny, like in the Antiques Barn. Fine paintings hung on the wall. Beautiful tables, dressers, armoires, and other furniture from various eras had been gathered in small groupings, allowing for viewing from all sides. Exotic carpets from the Middle East and Southwest lay over the hardwood floor. Gorgeous vases with fresh flowers and other decorations added to the feel of a European home. Each vignette reeked of taste and reserve, very out of place in a town considered on the verge of West Texas. Which is what intrigued Mina, when the shop's owner seemed prone to excess in the way she lived her life.

Oh crap, she'd already donated. Mina searched for a response. "Oh, I'm sure they just forgot. I'm seeing them this evening and I'll be sure to let them know to look for it."

Irritation flickered across her perfectly made up features. She crossed her arms at her ample chest. "You tell them I'm still taking the write-off for the donation, even if they've lost it. A vintage MontBlanc pen is not something you *just forget*."

"Sure." Mina scrambled for something leading to Wayne's death. "I better get back to the Cup. It's been really busy since everyone's been coming in wanting gossip on Wayne Beedy's death, what with him being found in my shed and everything." Had anger tightened Stacey's jaw for the barest second? Or fear? Mina dug deep in her heart for the innocence she'd feign for her coming question. "Oh, but I heard you hung out with him quite a bit?"

Stacey's mouth flared into an oval and she tried to get some words out, but all that emerged were choked grunts. Her face turned an unattractive blotchy red.

Inwardly, Mina smirked. "I'm sorry. He must've meant a lot to you."

"I did not *hang out* with Wayne Beedy."

Mina took a step back with the force of Stacey's words. Interesting Stacey hadn't said she didn't *know* Wayne Beedy. She specifically said they didn't hang out.

She seemed to realize the volume of her words told more than they should. Stacey smoothed her hair, adjusted the waistband of her linen skirt. "Who told you I knew Wayne Beedy, of all people?" Despite her more modulated tones, fury lay behind it.

Mina waived an airy hand. "Oh, you know, I hear things at the Cup. Someone said they saw you in a car with him one day not too long ago." She tapped her index finger against her cheek. "I wish I could remember who. Ah, anyway, you know gossip.

People make up the strangest things. They could even say something crazy like you going over to Garrett's while he and I were separated in nothing but your mink coat." Mina shook her head in mock despair, but kept an eye on Stacey whose jaw slackened momentarily, enough to confirm the story in Mina's mind. *What a witch.*

"I would do no such thing." Her hands shook as she smoothed her hair back, now a sure tell Mina had rattled her.

"Oh, I know, Stacey. Garrett's a handsome man, but everyone knows he's married to The Meanest Girl West of the Mississippi, right?" Mina cackled.

All color drained from Stacey's face. "Are you threatening me?"

Mina slapped her hand to her chest. "Me? Threatening you? Did I shout I'd kill you or something?" She mimicked Stacey's gracious, condescending manner. "Goodness, how did we even get here? I was saying people make up the craziest things for gossip purposes. I'm sure Chief Ruiz will be talking to everyone who knew Wayne. Lucky for me, Garret and I were at home that night."

"OP and I were also," she said, a shade too quickly. Stacey's hand came to her mouth, but then she moved it so her index finger covered her lips. Guilt? Or just not wanting to say more?

"Since you didn't know Wayne, I'm sure the Chief has no reason to question you. My regards to OP." Like Mina wouldn't see him in the morning anyway. She spun on her heel and headed for the door. Over her shoulder, she said, "Don't worry, I'll make sure they find the pen."

The door closed behind her with a snap that rattled the inset window. Mina didn't bother to look back. Between her shoulder blades a warmth grew as if Stacey's laser stare started to cut a hole. *Let her chew on our little talk.* Mina had gotten a two-for out of it. Not only had she informed Stacey her little trip to the Shaffer's Ranch had been discovered, but if her people-reading skills were worth a dime, Stacey not only knew Wayne Beedy, but his death scared the bejeezus out of her.

A bounce to her step, Mina swung her Cowboy Chic Boutique bag and whistled the latest Country Swing Kings release, her heart the lightest it'd been in years. Finally, things looked up. She and Garrett were back on track, though they'd need to talk about Stacy's visit. Wayne's actions may have cost her a pretty penny, but she remained on track to pay off the Cup in five years. And maybe, just maybe, she could do this ghost thing. She put her hand on the cafe door's push bar.

"Mina!"

She turned to see Janice Pinkerton scurrying from the vicinity of the Hairport Styling Salon across the street, then stepped away from the door as a couple exited. "Hey there, neighbor."

The older woman stopped once she achieved the shade of the Cup's awning. Though the hot late-summer wind tossed Mina's ponytail over her shoulder, Janice's short, gray cap didn't budge, even when she looked left and right as if ready to divulge she knew who killed Kennedy.

"What's up?" Mina prayed her prompt would get Janice to hurry, it still had to be one hundred in the shade.

"Matt called."

Mina's stomach clenched. If Dew Drop Police's day shift supervisor called his mamma, something big happened.

"He told me they arrested Brian Majors for Wayne Beedy's murder."

SIXTEEN

She was cutting it close. Mina pulled her truck into Doc Bannister's driveway minutes before she was due to pick up the kids. Clara already called to report she'd stay another night with Brittany in Fort Worth and the kids needed clothing for tomorrow. Chief Ruiz reported the kids' bedrooms hadn't been touched, mercifully. At least Brian resided in the Dew Drop jail for now and couldn't do any more damage. Bonus? They'd solved Wayne's murder and she was off the hook with the annoying ghost.

As she emerged past the last of the enormous pampas grass tussocks, she spied a silver hatchback sedan parked in the carport. Alarmed, Mina stopped her pickup. Clara drove an older-model sedan, and by all accounts should be one hundred miles away in

Fort Worth. She grabbed her phone from the console to call 911.

A flash from the window on the screen door halted her thumb. A woman emerged and skipped down the two short steps, tucking something under her arm. She wore a severe black suit, hair clipped back in a low pony tail. Laura Horne.

Why would Laura be here? Mina eased off the brake.

Laura's head whipped toward Mina's truck. She opened the driver's door of her car, tossed in whatever had been under her arm, and waited in the door's apex.

Mina stopped her slow roll and parked next to the sedan under the carport. She hopped down, swung her door shut behind her. "Didn't think I'd see anyone here."

"Brittany hadn't provided Kinley and Trace's immunization records. I called her and she told me where to find them." She crossed her arms at her chest. Despite the color flagging her cheeks, her nose rose higher as if daring Mina to contradict her.

Immunization records? Laura may be a stickler for the rules, but really? And why did Laura look more like a schoolgirl caught smoking than a school principal? Bah. Mina needed to get the clothing and move along. "I'm picking up some clothes for the kids."

"Brittany said they'd be staying with you for another night." Laura held herself stiff as barn board, words grating from between her lips.

An awkward silence stretched. Mina started around the silver car. "Well, I'll head inside. Gotta get the kids picked up in a couple."

Laura couldn't have appeared more relieved. The slam of the sedan's door and the quiet whirr of her eco-engine were Mina's only farewell.

Geez. And I have a rep for being rude. She inserted the key Clara had given her into the doorknob and pushed the door open. Good grief. As if Brian Majors hadn't done enough, the crime scene people sure hadn't cleaned up the mess. With the drapes pushed to the side to allow maximum light, the words on the walls and the destruction of furniture took her breath away. How could someone be so ugly to do something like this?

A painted white side cabinet inside the door had a fine, black dust covering its top. Fingerprint powder. Ugh. What a mess. She gathered a set of clothing for each of the kids from their rooms, both mercifully free of Brian's wrath. With a push of the lock button on the knob, she pulled the door shut behind her. Wait. How did Laura get in? Did she break in or have a key? Why would she have a key? Maybe Brittany told her where she'd hidden one.

Mina started down the steps when a manila envelope snagged her attention. It lay on the carport's concrete, under where Laura's car had been.

Tingling pricked her nape. Mina crept forward, as if she'd be caught without a hall pass and sent to the principal's office. Silly. The shot records. Laura probably dropped them.

Or it could've been under Laura's car and it was something the crime scene people dropped. Mina ran the envelope through her hands. Bulky, but flexible. Paper, numerous folded sheets if she had a guess. She'd need to know who to give it to, right? She flexed the silver clasp with one of her barely-there nails, lifted the flap and peered inside.

Envelopes, maybe ten or twelve in total. Not shot records. Maybe threats from Brian? She pulled one out. No address, only a name, 'Brittany' in tidy, feminine script. Crime scene techs must've dropped it. Though she should've put the envelope back in the larger one, every fiber of her being screamed to open it. She caved.

The neatly folded paper inside bore the same script as its outer shell.

Dearest Bri,

It's the long brown of August in Dew Drop. I

study the withering grass and flowers, parched by the lack of what they need most. I can't help comparing myself to these poor plants. I know now isn't the time for us to discuss the future. Brian is still dragging you through court and my heart breaks for you and the children. Life is unfair. In a fair world, we could be together—

Good gravy. A love letter!

—but it is conspiring against us for now. I count the days, the hours, the minutes until you move back to Dew Drop. It is still a community I fear that would be unaccepting of us, but even being with you in secret is better than never experiencing the love we share ever again.

Mina scanned the remaining two paragraphs to the signature. A bare letter, *L*. It had to be Laura. Laura who wrote the letter. Laura who dropped the manila envelope after retrieving it from Brittany's house.

Mina folded the paper with precision and tucked it back in its carrier. Unable to control her impulse, her fingers fished for another letter. This time it was only the paper, unevenly folded. She shouldn't read it. Yet her fingers still spread it out. Not a love letter this time. Block letters from what looked like magazines were pasted on the paper.

Bitch,

Nice opening. Mina snorted.

I bet their are alot of people who would like to know about you being lezbians. If you don't want them to find out, put $10000 in a paper bag and put it under the big rock at Hwy 16 and CR 495. I'm sure the judge would like to know to.

Brittany and Laura were being blackmailed. Mina's thoughts flew from the kids to the two women to Brittany plunging off Highway 16 to near death. Mina looked back at the page, but they hadn't signed it. She laughed at herself. Who signed a blackmail note? Her gaze zeroed in on her hand and she wanted to slap the back of her head for her stupidity. Now *her* fingerprints were on it.

She folded it back and deposited the letter into the larger envelope, then bent the clasp over the flap to secure it. She tapped the bottom corner against her calf as she considered what to do with the dynamite.

Had Laura entered with a key, essentially with Brittany's permission? Or had she broken in to get it? It was pretty easy to jimmy a lock in a doorknob, right?

She moved to the house's entry. The wood on the door had multiple indentations where it had been pried, but the lock itself didn't have any marks on it, as if someone had tried to force it open with a tool.

She couldn't tell if Laura had added her own marks to those Brian put there when he forced open the door yesterday.

A male voice said in her ear, "What are you doing?"

SEVENTEEN

Mina jumped sideways from the voice, heart crawling to get out of her throat, allowing only a strangled scream. She whirled and prepared to knee the jerk in the junk.

Wayne Beedy stood at her side studying the door near its knob.

"For the love of all that's holy, do *not* sneak up on me anymore."

He straightened and had the gall to look offended. "I didn't sneak up on you. I called your name. You didn't respond and I came over to see what you were looking at."

Finally, her heart had slowed to a less-than-coronary level. "The marks Brian Majors left on the door when he broke in."

"What'd he do?"

"You're a ghost. Go look." She scooped up the small duffle and the envelope she'd dropped preparing to defend herself. *Annoying as much in death as in life.*

Though she said it in jest, she goggled when Wayne stepped though the brick wall next to the door. He emerged a couple of seconds later. "Yep, that's Brian, alright," he said with a hearty laugh.

Her gaze narrowed on Wayne. "How do you know him?"

He turned his head away from her, as if upset he'd spoken, and remained silent for several moments. Then he said, "He moved to a rent house in Santo when Brittany brought the kids back to Dew Drop."

Only ten miles north up the road. "It doesn't explain how you know him."

He jutted his chin out. "He likes to tweek once in a while. I met him through some friends."

"Tweek?"

"Do meth." His eyes slid away from hers.

Oh boy. "How did you know Brittany? Were y'all dating?"

"I never met her." The guilt written plain as day on his face revealed him as a rotten liar.

Pulling teeth from an unsedated greased pig would be easier than getting the truth from Wayne.

"You said you were headed here when you were killed. Why would Brian kill you, then?"

"Brian killed me?" He jaw hung slack.

"They arrested him for your murder this afternoon." She crossed her arms at her chest. "Look, I really don't care why he did it. They arrested your murderer. I'm saging the house this afternoon, so you won't be able to come in uninvited." A little bit of a lie, since she needed Lacey to show her the ropes, but hopefully it would keep the jerk out. "Go into the light or whatever you need to do. I'm done." She stomped to her truck and yanked open the door, slid the envelope under the console, tossed the bag in back, then climbed in.

He appeared at her side in the passenger seat. "He didn't kill me. I know it." His tone crossed from despair to anger.

"I thought you didn't see it." She shook her head. "Doesn't matter. The Texas Rangers think they've found enough to charge him with murder. Unless you have a reason to tell me why he didn't, like if you know who did, then I suggest you go off to your next life, wherever that may be." She started the truck. "Regardless, get out. I have to pick up my kid. And don't you approach him in the future. I'm a Flannigan. I'll figure out how to make sure your next life is unhappier than you think it's going to be." Maybe he'd believe she could do it, too.

His jaw firmed under the shadowy, scrubby beard he'd never have to shave again. "He didn't kill me. I know it."

"You already said that. Unless you want to stop lying to me, I'm not interested." She put the truck in reverse and into the sunlight.

He didn't speak until she reached the end of the driveway. "Okay. I went to Brian's house after I escaped."

She did *not* have time for this. Yet, she put the truck in park, then twisted toward him, resting her elbow on the steering wheel. "And?"

"Mom would've kicked me out, plus it's the first place they'd try. Everly and Cathy would've been second, and they would've kicked me out, too," he said bitterly. "Few people knew Brian and I knew each other. He knows what I'm—I *was*—going through with Everly and Cathy not letting me see my kids. But he told me I couldn't stay. If they found me at his apartment, there'd be no way he'd ever get to see his kids again, that Brittany would make sure." Desperately his eyes searched hers. "We were friends. He wouldn't kill me." His voice trailed off, forlorn, as if he'd talked himself into the betrayal.

Though it pained her, she believed him. And

even pitied him a bit, which couldn't have shocked her more. To have no one to run to when you need it most must be horrible. Even if she and Sunny weren't talking right now, she'd still have Sunny's back and Sunny hers. Yet... "You still haven't told me how you knew Brittany."

"I told you. She wouldn't have done it." There might as well be a neon sign over his head flashing 'BS ARTIST'.

Whatever empathy he'd created evaporated with his evasion. "Whatever. You've heard me. They caught your murderer. Now scram." Mina looked both ways for traffic and when she turned back to emphasize her get lost mantra, no Wayne remained.

Only the sad, ghost-thin words of, "He didn't do it. I know it."

Persistent cuss.

A few minutes later, she pulled into the school parking lot next to Laura's car, then retrieved the envelope from under her armrest console. She stared at the Fellowship Church's shiny new administration building across the school's playground. How would Pastor Davis take something like this? The love letters could ruin Laura and Brittany, who taught fourth grade in Palo Pinto to the north. Too many prejudices remained in this tiny community. Hadn't the Flannigans been shunned by some, derided and laughed at by others in this town? Like she'd been as a child. Like she'd be if her power now became known? How Laura and Brittany wanted to live their lives was their own decision. No one deserved to be shunned for their choice of life partner.

But what to do about the blackmail letter? Who could've sent it? Brian? No. He'd have brought up Brittany and Laura's relationship to the judge in the hope it would cause trouble. Not every judge in the State of Texas believed the gay lifestyle a reason to lose custody of children, but the mere chance of it happening could be enough for Brittany or Laura to pay it. What an awful rock and an equally terrible hard place.

Not your business, Mina. Unless you want to join Nosey Turner in the gossip corner. She hopped out of the truck, secure in her heart she was doing the right thing.

Someone buzzed her through to the administration office, and Mina stopped at the half wall. "Hi, Mrs. Taylor. Is Laura in?"

The secretary, who'd been elderly when Mina started at the old school across town, nodded her head. She lifted the handset and said, "Let me see if she's free." Or had Mina been young enough the woman merely looked old to young eyes? Mrs. Taylor put the phone receiver back in its cradle. "She'll be a minute, dear. How's the Tea Cup? That chocolate pecan pie with bourbon whipped cream is the best I've ever had." She smacked her lips, sugar lust lighting her eyes.

"Thanks. Been working on some new recipes for fall and Christmas."

"Ooh, what?"

"Still working on them, so I'm not sharing any secrets." When Mrs. Taylor slumped a little in apparent disappointment, Mina added, "But I can say it involves maple syrup." She tossed a wink on top for good measure.

Laura opened her door. "What can I do for you Mina?" The way she stood in the opening, her jaw clenched so hard a muscle sawed back and forth, didn't brook invitation into the inner sanctum. She spied the envelope in Mina's hand and her nostrils flared. She even widened her stance a bit as if preparing for battle.

Like it would keep Mina from her objective. "It's personal, if you don't mind." Mina followed the principal into the office when she swept her arm wide and spun on her heel.

Laura stood behind her desk and assumed a veneer of calm. The shaking hands she tried to hide by crossing her arms across her chest gave away her fury or fear or both. The will it took for the principal to not stare at the envelope in Mina's hands was palpable.

Who would blame the woman? Mina had been a mostly horrible person for many years. Laura could only believe the worst. "Here are the shot records. You must've dropped them before you left." She placed the envelope in the middle of the principal's desk.

"Thank you." The words had been spoken through lips pursed tight. It was a wonder they didn't snap like rubber bands.

Mina needed her to know. Not to be mean, but so Laura understood she didn't have anything to fear from Mina. "I had to look inside to see if it was the shot records or something the crime scene people dropped yesterday."

Laura's face paled, but her nose tilted even higher. "You read them?"

Mina jerked a nod. "One." A tiny lie wouldn't matter. "I needed to know who to give it to. Once I figured out I'd found the shot records, I didn't go any further. That's personal. No one's business but the people involved." Mina pivoted on her sneakered heel. Once through the door, she closed it quietly behind her.

EIGHTEEN

"Thanks, Mina." Clara's sweet blue eyes peered through the service window at the Cup. It was Saturday just after noon.

Mina stopped on her way to refill Chief Ruiz's glass of sweet tea. "You *can* stop now, you know." Kinley and Trace had stayed the last three nights with the Garretts, since Clara returned from Fort Worth late yesterday. Clara planned to leave early to pick up Brittany and Mina would bring the children to Clara's house. Not only did Brittany still need someone to help her recuperate, but they couldn't go back to Doc Bannister's until cleaned up. Right now, the kids should be finishing up at Jake's baseball game.

"No, I really *can't* stop. You've been working overtime to make up for me not being here. And you kept the kids." A sheen grew in Clara's eyes, quickly blinked away.

Mina put her full pitcher on the counter with a laugh. "Jimmy and I managed well enough and you know I can do breakfast in my sleep since you taught me how. Smother my biscuits with enough gravy and customers think they're yours." She sobered. "If it hadn't been for you, I never would've been able to run this restaurant. Consider it payback. And I'm sure the kids will be happy for her to come home."

Clara's mouth pursed. "She'd have her own house to go home to if it hadn't been for Brian."

Rageena stuck a ticket on the silver order wheel. "Glad to have you back, Clara," she said, then moved off to the register to ring up Pastor Davis and his wife. *Poor thing. I wonder if she knows the whole town is talking about his supposed affair with his secretary?*

Mina moved on, down to the end of the counter where Daniel sat, midway through today's chicken and dumplings special. She filled his cup with sweet tea. "How's the Beedy case going, Chief?"

The corners of his lips turned down. "Wish they had dumped him somewhere in the county." He took a sip of tea from an oversized, sweating plastic cup. "And I'm sorry I couldn't get you to you before David Pinkerton's mom did. You should've heard it from me. And it's why I'm telling you now. He's getting out this afternoon on a ridiculously low bond for the break-in at Brittany's and they're dropping the murder charges. Make sure you get the surveillance system in as soon as possible. He knows you told me about seeing him the day he vandalized the house." Daniel sought her gaze with troubled eyes. "He's not a nice person. I'm going to call Brittany to make sure she knows. I'm not sure what he'll do next."

Mina shivered, recalling the violent destruction at Doc Bannister's house. Surely Brian wouldn't come after her? "I'll get Garrett on it. He got the one installed at the house the day we found Wayne in the shed." She was still getting used to the electronic alarm keypad and locks on the doors leading outside. Another system in the Cup would drive her crazy. All in a town where people usually locked their homes only during the Iced Tea Festival when throngs of visitors came for the music, art, and final donation to the Wounded Warrior Foundation at the closing ceremony. "Not enough evidence?"

He tucked away the last bite of dumpling on a sigh. "It was only the tire track. I wouldn't have arrested him. Too many of those tires on trucks across Texas, but the Rangers thought they may be able to get him to confess in the interrogation. I could've told them he would lawyer up quick as a flash. He's too smart for his own good." Daniel snapped his fingers, then dug in his back pocket.

"You know it goes on your bill. I'll send it soon," Mina said, fully intending not to do so.

His fond smile under the bushy mustache warmed her. "See you do. But I wasn't reaching for my wallet." He put a rectangle of paper on the counter and slid it toward her with his fingers. "Wanted to make sure you knew what Majors looked like since he isn't a Dew Drop native."

"I've never seen him." She picked up the photo printed on paper in simple black and white. Her breath caught in her throat at the fury radiating from his dark eyes, the mean set of his mouth. With a height chart behind him and a towel around his neck, it had to be a mug shot. She handed it back, squishing the desire to wash her hands. "Thanks."

"Just trying to keep you safe." He tucked it back in his pocket. "And see you put up the security system soon."

Any comfort given by his earlier grin evaporated with his last sentence. Tingles danced along her spine, raising hair on her arms. Another sign? No. More like she couldn't afford to clean up a similar destruction in her restaurant. She said an unusual silent prayer, grateful Garrett scheduled installation for tomorrow.

She picked up Daniel's plate and headed to the service door on the other side of the counter. The bell over the door heralded a late lunch visitor and she turned to welcome the customer. Laura Horne walked toward her and Mina almost dropped the plate in her hand. Laura had been back in town now since early summer without coming into the Cup. This had to be about the letters. Mina braced for a confrontation.

"Hello." A self-deprecating curve crossed her lips. She gestured to the dessert cooler under the cash register. "Could I get a couple of pies? I'd like to treat the staff." A friendly tone? From Laura? On a Saturday?

Mina decided not to question providence. She hurried through the service door to deposit the Chief's plate, then returned and matched Laura's casual attitude. "Sure. What would you like? We've got at least one of every kind, except for the chocolate pecan. It usually sells out, so you have to get in early or give an advance order."

"Shoot. Mrs. Taylor said it was the best pie she'd ever had." Laura bent to examine the sweets. Light bounced off strands of gray in her dark blonde hair. She straightened. "I'll have to be happy with a banana cream, pecan, and deep-dish apple."

Mina turned and assembled three cardboard pie

boxes, then set Laura's selections to the side of the register and rang up the total. Smiles wreathed the woman's face, as if they'd been friends forever. Surely it couldn't just be because Mina essentially told Laura she didn't care about her sexual orientation? But maybe it was. It couldn't be easy to be gay in small town like Dew Drop.

Laura fished in her purse for her wallet, then handed Mina some bills. After Mina handed her change back, Laura slid the stacked boxes from the counter and into her hands.

Mina hurried around the pie cooler. "Here, let me get the door for you. Do you need help with your car?"

Laura stopped before she stepped through the opening and jangled her keys dangling in one hand. "The trunk will open automatically. Thank you, Mina. You've been wonderful."

This conversation didn't sound much like pies at all. Mina shrugged. "It's pie."

"That too." With a downward jerk of her chin, Laura left the Cup, sensible heels clicking on the concrete.

Mina allowed the door to swing shut aided by its hydraulic arm. She tracked Laura through the front windows to the compact silver hatchback. As she approached the vehicle's rear, the trunk's back window rose. She deposited the pies, shut it and got into her car with a short, tentative wave.

Mina jerked back, not believing Laura would've looked for her. Snowballs in hell were surely freezing today. If someone had told her Horrible Horne would be friendly toward her, Mina would've have scoffed.

Clara appeared at Mina's side, wiping her hands on a dishtowel and tracking the retreating car with narrowed eyes. "What did that woman want?" The venom in the cook's voice caught Mina off guard. Usually, Clara was the picture of cheer, their very own Mrs. Claus.

"She only bought some pies."

Clara looked at her hands as the fabric wrung through them and it confirmed Mina's suspicions.

She knew about Brittany and Laura and didn't approve.

NINETEEN

Later that evening, Mina, knocked on Clara's front door and waited for an answer. Kinley and Trace stood next to her. Since her large sedan sat in the carport, Clara had to be back from Fort Worth with Brittany. Mina pushed the doorbell again, then scanned the windows. Desperate to reach the light, moths tapped against the windows of what should be the living room.

"Try the door," Kinley said.

It wasn't polite to walk on into a house without an announcement, one of many courtesies drummed into her head by Granma. But the kids were family, right? Mina twisted the knob and found it locked. "Stay here in case your auntie or mamma comes to the door. I'll go around back." She left the children on the concrete stoop and rounded the corner. Voices carried from the back.

"You need to stop seeing her," Clara said. Instead of anger, her words carried defeat.

Shamefully, Mina stopped before she revealed herself.

"You know I can't, Clara." The soft tones could've only come from Brittany. "I love her."

"But this whole blackmail thing with Wayne would never have happened—"

"You don't know for sure. If it wasn't him, it might have been someone else."

Blackmail? Wayne? Mina scoffed at her initial surprise. After all, he'd blackmailed her into finding his killer. Why would she be surprised he'd blackmailed Brittany and Laura.

Clara *humphed.* "Do you think Brian knew, too?"

"I don't know. Maybe he put him up to it."

"We'll never know now he's dead. I just hope the police— What was that sound?"

Clara's sharp words prompted Mina from her hiding place. "Hello?" she cried out as she made the corner. "Anyone here? Oh—there y'all are."

Clara rose from her seat on a plastic patio chair. A younger woman reclined on a lounge chair, dark rings of bruising under her weary eyes, an arm casted and strapped in a sling. She struggled to rise, imitating her aunt's southern courtesy with the appearance of guests.

"Please, stay seated," Mina said. "I'll go get the kids."

Clara waved Mina toward one of the empty chairs. "Have a seat. I forgot I hadn't unlocked the front door. I'll let the kids in." She bustled into the small brick house through a sliding glass door.

It was a testament to Clara's agitation that she didn't make the introductions. Mina slid down into a brown plastic adirondack chair still warm from the afternoon sun and peered at the woman who could only be a couple of years older than herself. "I'm Mina. I'll take it by the bandages, you're Brittany?"

She lifted her casted arm in its sling and winced. "Guilty." Bruises, setting toward greens and yellows stood out on her face, but the spectacular black eyes from the still-bandaged wound on her forehead would take its sweet time to fade.

The silence had grown and it was Mina's conversation turn. "I'm glad you're going to be okay." She covered her wince at the stupid platitude with a smile.

"Someday." The tight word rang with restrained pain.

Kinley and Trace flew through the door with cries of "Mama!"

"Watch now. She's still hurt. Be gentle," Clara said from the doorway.

The youngsters held up as they reached their mother. Kinley started crying, then Trace joined in with piteous wails of his own.

"Come here, my loves." Brittany sat up a little and wrapped her unbandaged arm around them both. The grimace on her face as she pressed them close testified to her agony, but also her love. "Shh. Don't cry. I'm okay." She stroked their hair, murmured over and over until the children settled. Finally, she leaned back and leveled a perfect mom-look. "Were you good for Miss Shaffer?"

Both nodded, mute.

"Good. Is your homework done, young lady?" Again, Kinley nodded, then wiped under her nose.

"Then go on and get ready for bed. I'll be there in a couple of minutes to tuck you both in."

The two youngsters headed off, their slow steps saying they didn't want to leave her yet, but knew better than to argue.

Clara appeared, glass in hand. "Sweet tea?"

Normally, Mina wouldn't have accepted the sugar-laden beverage this late in the evening. Granma's manners wouldn't allow such a discourtesy, so she accepted it and took a sip, allowing the icy-sweet tea to slide down her throat. The house sat on a small rise big enough to see the horizon over the scrub oak.

The three sat in silence on Clara's back patio for several minutes as the sun slid itself over the edge of the world, turning the scant clouds to flames reaching into the dark of night. During the time, Mina covertly examined Brittany, trying to discern if she could've killed Wayne. Like most females in this part of the world during this time of year, she'd pulled her long, thick mahogany hair off her neck. She'd be pretty tall, but then everyone else in the world could top Mina's own scant five feet. Jeans shorts and a simple button-up tank didn't scream 'killer.' What did a murderer look like anyway? For it certainly could've been Brittany if she knew Wayne to be her blackmailer. And what wouldn't Mina do herself to protect Jake? Or her sisters? Or Garrett?

Mina finally broke into the cicada's song. "Thanks for the tea. I need to be getting back." She set her glass on the table and began to rise.

"Please don't leave yet," Brittany said. "I've been sitting here figuring out how to thank you."

"You already did. Your kids behaved beautifully." The more she'd studied Kinley, her initial snootiness became something Mina understood. The girl came from a large city to a small town where everyone knew each other, a complete culture shift. The defensive behavior had evaporated after the first night. "They did exactly what I asked with no sass. It's getting harder and harder to find in kids today."

"It wasn't what I meant, but thank you. It's been hard the last year. Brian has...well, he's difficult. And the kids sometimes don't understand." Her gaze flicked to her lap. "What I meant was about—"

"She meant letting me go to stay with her." Clara's words rang out overloud into the gathering dusk.

"Clara, that's not what I meant."

"Brittany, I don't think..."

"She *knows*, Clara."

"I...I..." Clara floundered, then stumbled to a halt and hung her head in her cook-worn hands.

Oh boy. How to exit gracefully—

"If you want, the kids and I can find somewhere else to live. I'm sorry I'm such an embarrassment to you." Brittany's voice had started small, but had grown with confidence.

"No," Clara said on a gasp. "You can't leave here."

"I'm not going to stay here if who I am is not wanted or respected."

"It's not me. It's a small town. People won't understand. They may even fire you in Palo Pinto."

Bright red spots appeared in Brittany's wan features. "Too bad. I'll find somewhere who will rent to me. And then I'll look a couple of towns over for another teaching position."

"Pardon me for interrupting," Mina said. "I do think you should remain with Clara until you recover, since Brian's getting out of jail-maybe already has. Chief Ruiz was very adamant he's a violent person." Dang it. She probably should've bitten her tongue and not gotten involved. "I shouldn't tell you what to do. It's none of my business."

All color drained from Brittany's face. "He's getting out?" she asked on a barest whisper.

"Oh lord." That's what you get for poking your nose in people's business. No more eavesdropping and gossip. "Chief Ruiz said he'd call you to let you know. I'm sorry."

"I'm sure he called. I've got a bazillion messages to listen to." She covered her eyes with her hand and sobbed a laugh. "Just when I think he's finally done enough to keep himself in trouble, he gets out of it again."

Clara's fist pounded on the table. "Let him come here. I'll fill his butt so full of buckshot, it'll take a dump truck to haul him around." The ferociousness in Clara's tone indicated she'd relish loading up on 12-gauge ammo and making good on the threat.

"I don't want a loaded gun in the house." Brittany

wiped tears away with her good hand. "There's been too much violence already. The kids don't need more." She turned to Mina, warmth in her hazel gaze. "Thank you for letting me know." Her phone, which sat on a glass side table next to her, rang. She picked it up with an apologetic grimace. "Pardon me. Hello? Hi, Sheriff Potts. No, right now's fine." As she listened, the muscles in her body tightened. "It was, was it? I will absolutely come in tomorrow." She ended the call, jaw clenched, all apparent pain and fatigue replaced by anger and agitation. "That's it. I'm done with trying to make nice with Brian for the kids." She slashed her unrestrained hand in the air. "The Sheriff suspects Brian cut my brake line."

Now there was the woman who would pull a trigger for Kinley and Trace.

TWENTY

Sunday morning dawned, warm but bearable. Mina sat on the back-porch swing, her preferred place to think, while listening to the world awaken around her. She sipped from her third cup of coffee and surveyed the birds wheeling through the dappled light stealing through the oak limbs.

The back door opened and the wood screen door's ancient spring *screeked* then slapped the door shut. "Thought I might find you out here." Garrett sat next to her. The old wood protested a bit while the chain groaned. They sat in companionable silence for a moment, each sipping the strong brew Mina adored.

"You didn't sleep well last night, did you?" Garrett finally said.

"That bad, huh?" If she'd gotten an hour, she'd be

surprised. Yesterday had been long and eventful, leaving much for her to consider. Wayne's steadfast belief Brian hadn't killed him. Brittany's call from the Palo Pinto Sheriff. Clara's distress about people finding out about Brittany and Laura. And then Stacey and Wayne. All bits of information without any connections.

"Lots of sighs and tossing. Got anything you want help with? Like the murder?"

She's related to Garrett her discovery of Brittany's blackmail last night. She had a twinge of guilt, because it wasn't her secret, but it was her husband after all. Then she'd told Garrett what she'd learned about Stacey Boyd and her alleged interactions with Wayne. For some reason, she kept her mouth closed about Stacey's visit to Garrett at the Shaffer Ranch. Suddenly, it didn't matter. Deep in her heart, Mina trusted he'd never be stupid enough to fall for that woman's charms.

Mina stared at a mockingbird perched on a branch, announcing to the world this was his patch of air. She drummed her fingers on the swing's arm. "I have a bunch of bits of information, but no connections."

Garrett pushed the swing a bit with his boot. "I still can't get over Stacey. She's fallen quite a bit if she and Wayne were knocking boots."

"Ain't that the truth." Mina still had a hard time believing they would have an affair, even after what Olivia divulged about the former beauty-queen's skanky ways.

"Then Brittany and Laura and the blackmail? She ought to just come out. I mean, Dew Drop's come a long way in a couple of years." He took a sip of his coffee and swallowed. "We even had a man buy one of the bachelors at the Library Benefit Auction."

The town had come pretty far, but it still had a way to go. "Brittany probably thinks it's not worth the chance. I'm sure her divorce is still on-going in Fort Worth. You don't know these days. And Brian could take her back to court at any time, like Shelby did with Mike, remember?" Garret's brother spent more in legal fees than he earned in a year to keep the same visitation for his kids.

"Ugh. It was awful." He sipped his coffee. "But now there's a couple of sticks in the spokes for the case of Brian murdering Wayne. Brittany and Stacey had the perfect excuse, and I'd say both barely had an alibi. Brittany could've snuck out after she settled the kids and OP usually has enough bourbon in him by nine P-M, Stacey could bring a brass band in the bedroom and he wouldn't wake up."

Mina nodded. Practically everyone knew OP's

penchant for a snoot full. "The more I think about it, the more suspects crop up and the less it looks like Brian. Brittany had motive. Clara and Laura would have reason, too. Even OP, if he believed his wife cheated on him."

Garrett's eyebrows rose. "Clara? Your cook? The one everyone refers to as Mrs. Claus because she's the sweetest thing since sugar?" He shook his head. "No one would believe it."

"You didn't see her face when she threatened to fill Brian's behind with buckshot if he showed his face around her house." Or when she twisted the towel in her hand when Mina mentioned Laura. She slid him a side eye. "I notice you didn't take up the banner for Laura or OP."

He huffed a laugh. "OP could definitely do it. As for Laura, I don't know her well." He sipped again from his oversized Shaffer Hardware cup. "She's always seemed so reserved. Don't they say 'still waters run deep'? Maybe she has it in her."

"I bet someone would do a lot for someone they loved. I know I would." *Murder? Sure.* Threaten her family, and Mina would gladly spend the rest of her life in jail if she could save them.

"The big question is, what do you tell Daniel?"

She pondered it, staring into her Cup-logoed coffee mug. "I can't see Brittany, Laura, or Clara shooting Wayne. Stacey's a stretch, even with her waiving a gun around. Brian's still on the short-list."

"And any other of Wayne's tweeked out friends. Who knows what mischief he got into before he got arrested?" He flipped his wrist to look at his watch then rose from the swing. "I'll get Jake going."

How she loved this man. "Thanks. Don't forget, today's the picnic."

Garrett's features twisted into a grimace. "Why do they plan these things in September when they know the Sunday will always be near one hundred degrees? I'm going to petition mom to get it changed to Spring."

"I'll be right behind you. She probably would have enough pull on the church board. "But at this time of year, they've got a pretty good chance it won't rain, except for an afternoon pop-up storm, so..." She shrugged.

His grumblings followed him inside, the screen door slapping shut behind him.

She rested back into the swing and pushed off with her bare toe. What *was* she going to do? Brian had been arrested, but they'd let him out. Plus, he had to be the prime suspect in Brittany's 'accident'. But then there were Clara, Brittany, Laura, Stacey, even OP, all with motive. All with motive only Mina knew, outside the people themselves.

She moved into the house, went through the motions of cooking breakfast. Clara had been too good to Mina to turn her in on mere speculation. Brittany was escaping an abusive spouse. To be honest, she might've called the Chief about the blackmail letters if it hadn't been for the repercussions on Clara, and Mina's sympathy for her niece.

Husband and child fed, all dressed, they left for church at a quarter to ten, Mina still gnawing on the problem. Each time she came to the idea of turning any of them in based on second-hand gossip and guestimation, it twisted her stomach. But the idea of keeping the information from Chief Ruiz and the law seemed equally unjust. Around and around the dilemma turned, like her insides.

She slid from the passenger seat of her husband's SUV and into the already baking Texas morning. Immediately, she lifted her ponytail from her neck. The sun hung in the cloudless eastern sky, its rays promising searing temperatures. The stiff wind from the southwest did nothing to alleviate the heat, merely heightening the blast-furnace feel. She scanned the church grounds and sighted the large tents and their numerous tables dressed with blue plastic table cloths. Why couldn't they hold the event in the congregation hall? The A/C would be a welcome addition. Outside, it'd be a miracle for sure if her pies held onto their meringues and the silent auction sheets didn't blow all the way to Oklahoma City.

Once inside the front doors of the Fellowship Church, her eyes took time to adjust to the dim interior. She'd moved pews when she got married to Garrett. The Shaffers sat on the right of the long rectangle, near the front. When she'd attended as a child, the Flannigans sat in the back left. That way no one could see them come late or leave early. Or even note if they'd been there at all.

Settled into the pew, low voices surrounded them as Mina scanned the wall display for the numbers, then reached for the hymnal. The voices grew and she looked over her shoulder at the unexpected noise level, Nosey Turner's the most distinct. Some people glanced in Mina's direction from their little clusters. She'd had hoped dead Wayne in her shed would've died down by now. Not like the Flannigans hadn't been the center of gossip in the past. She returned her attention to preparing for the service.

"Mina," Olivia whispered from over her shoulder.

Mina swiveled on the polished oak pew, hooking an elbow over the back, noting the concern in Olivia's expression as she perched on the edge of the seat behind her.

Before her friend could deliver the news people weren't letting go of the topic of Wayne being found in the Flannigan-Shaffer shed, Mina said, "Don't tell me. Pastor Davis and Lois are having an affair?" Not like it hadn't been a much-speculated topic overheard in the Cup during the last year with the sightings of them at lunch and dinner together without his wife. Mina caught the envy in the women's tones, though. The pastor was handsome in a slick, smiley, perfect-white-teeth kind of way which did nothing to stir Mina's feminine parts.

Olivia's mouth formed an oval. "No way! An affair?"

Mina snorted a laugh. "No. I'm sure everyone's still stuck on Wayne being found in my shed." She shrugged. "I've heard it enough at the Cup lately. I hoped maybe something else had happened to get me out of the headlines." Not really when so many shifted their eyes toward her.

Her friend swatted Mina's arm with a broad smile. "No. At least not yet."

It figured she wouldn't be so lucky. "Well, what's up?"

Olivia's amused features shifted back to worry, a small frown tugging between her brows. "I wanted to make sure you were okay. It must've been hard to hear about Clara."

A pit began to yaw in Mina's belly. "What?"

For several moments, Olivia's face slackened, then her eyes widened. "Good gracious, you *didn't* know. Clara turned herself in for Wayne Beedy's murder."

TWENTY-ONE

Clara? Mina still couldn't fathom her sweet cook would kill anyone, let alone Wayne, despite her earlier speculation. She stood on the edge of the picnic in the shade of a line of oaks, eyes trained on the festivities, but her thoughts were a million miles away. Well, maybe three miles away and centered on a friend who was undoubtedly trying to do what she believed to be right.

She shook her head and surveyed the crowd, which had far surpassed last year's, largely due to the new pastor bringing in more to the flock. Nosey, Lois, and Garrett's mother, Irene, had huddled into a group by the silent auction tables. Olivia manned the barbecue meat table. Despite the crazy heat, the auction moved smoothly. Mina's eyes lit on what seemed like half the town, Mrs. Taylor from the school sat with other older church members, while the Youth Ministry participants served them lunch. Laura had been circled by a cluster of parents, no doubt wanting to curry favor with the head elementary administrator. No Brittany. Understandable considering the circumstances.

"Penny for them," a familiar female voice said.

Mina shouldn't have been surprised to see her youngest sister, Lacey, standing next to her. She had a habit of turning up at important moments. Lacey looked cool and gorgeous as always, half gypsy, half cowgirl, all independent spirit in her floaty short skirt, embroidered boots, layers of jewelry and straw hat. Most would never guess them to be related. More than half a foot taller and several cup sizes larger, plus thick curling black hair, Lacey stood out and over her much shorter, auburn-haired munchkin of an older sibling. A sharp pang of envy shot through Mina. She ruthlessly suppressed it. Mina loved her sister, and had too many of her own blessings to count. Plus, Lacey had her own problems.

Mina shook off the unexpected appearance and said into the growing silence, "Clara was arrested for Wayne Beedy's murder."

"I heard. I wonder how long it will take Chief Ruiz to discover Clara didn't do it."

Her sister's matter of fact tone caused Mina's heart to bump up a notch. "Did you see something?"

"Now you believe in the Flannigan Gift?" The mocking grin slid across her generous lips with the old argument. She didn't wait for an answer. "I know you do *now*. But I didn't use the Gift. Good old common sense told me. The woman could no more kill someone than I'm the President of these United States."

The hope bubble burst. If Lacey had just seen something, a clue of which way to go, who to start investigating to get Clara off the hook. But that wasn't Mina's luck. Then something Lacey said niggled at her. "I do now? So, you could see I believe in the Gift?"

"Funny. I *did* see that a couple of days ago. Ghosts, huh? Granma always said you had a Gift but you rejected it when you were young."

Nosey Turner had left her group and circled like a falling leaf, closer with each pass, avid curiosity lighting her eyes.

Ugh. Can't that woman leave well enough alone? Mina turned to her sister. "Can you take us to the house?" It'd be better to have this talk without prying ears.

Lacey cut a side-eye with a grin. "Sure."

During the short walk to Lacey's battered

pickup, Mina texted Garrett. Across the church lawn she saw him pull his phone from his pocket, look at it then scan for her. He nodded and waved.

A couple of seconds later, her phone beeped, indicating a text. *You look beautiful in that dress. I want to eat you up.*

Mina tucked her phone back into her purse, her heart floating. He'd never sent her something like that before. She made a mental note to thank Olivia when she saw her next.

When Mina opened the door to Lacey's truck, she had to shove aside the crumpled Whataburger bags and stained coveralls, text books and a myriad of other things. Mina couldn't stand a cluttered car, but her heart wasn't in the argument today. More pressing issues loomed. Besides, the ride to the house concluded almost as soon as it started. At least Lacey left the windows up and turned on the air conditioning. The crazy girl loved the searing summer temperatures.

At the house, Mina exchanged her pretty, but damp, dress for more reasonable clothing, shorts and a Tea Cup t-shirt. Perhaps she'd join Garrett's campaign to move the picnic to a cooler time of year.

When she returned downstairs, Lacey had already set out the items needed for the smudging. Of course she had. While Mina had once looked upon the practice as weird and embarrassing, she'd do it daily if it kept spirits out of her house.

Lacey looked up from the vast expanse of walnut dining table. "I'll make sure you get more sage. With work and the new semester starting, I haven't had time to get out here as often as I'd have liked. I told Jake to call me if there was a problem he couldn't handle."

Though innocent, Lacey's statement might as well have cut out Mina's heart. "I want to be jealous Jake went to you. But I did that. I should've been a better mom." Tears leapt to her eyes but she pushed them back. "Thank you for helping him." She choked the words out around a boulder in her throat.

"I didn't mean to hurt you." Lacey came around the table's corner and wrapped her arms around Mina's shoulders, squeezing her tight.

The tears leaked out until they became a shower. She leaned into Lacey, crying for the time she'd spent being stupid and mean and a control freak. Finally, she reigned in her tears. Not productive. She sucked in a big breath. A lot of the tension had fallen from her shoulders and a sense of peace settled in.

"You're not a bad mom, you know," her sister murmured into Mina's hair. "He loves you so much. He's just glad he has someone to talk to about this now besides me. Speaking of, how did he get a Gift? I thought only the Flannigan *women* got it?"

Mina disengaged herself and dabbed at her cheeks and nose with a tissue snagged from a nearby box. "I know, right? It's what Granma always said." She shrugged. "But if what we can do is real, who's to say it follows the rules?"

"Good point. I guess we'll never know."

"Shoot. I've been so wrapped up in me, I never asked you how things are going."

Lacey paused from closing a door on the sideboard where she stored her saging supplies. "Classes are going well. I think I'll be able to stay on the dean's list with my schedule. Spring will be harder as I head to graduation." She'd need every 'A' she could muster to get into veterinary school. Especially since she'd insisted she do it on her own, even when Mina and Garrett offered to co-sign on student loans.

A small bubble of pride grew in Mina's heart. "You've worked hard to get where you are. And we're all proud of you. How's work?'

"Doc Holty is tough, but I'm learning tons. If I ever know a quarter of what he knows about animals, I'll be happy." Lacey picked up the abalone shell from the dining table, it's bundled white sage resting inside, one end burned from prior use. Next, she tucked the bundle of three crow feathers she'd use to distribute the sage smoke under the shell in her hand.

Wait for it. "And with Walker? How's that going?"

Lacey stilled. Color flooded her chest above her frilly cotton tank top, then rose up her neck, depositing bright pink in her cheeks.

Whoa. Direct hit. Never before had Mina been able to score one on Lacey. The Sight had often afforded her youngest sister information no one else in the family knew and she'd had no problem with using it to blackmail her way out of trouble. Lacey thought Mina wasn't aware of the hunky young fireman from Abilene, Walker Evans. Maybe Nosey Turner, related to Walker's family, had her uses after all.

Lacey's eyes narrowed. "Jake. Jake told you."

Why would Jake be talking to Mina about his aunt's love life? Mina smirked. "Maybe. Maybe not."

Irritation flashed across Lacey's features then she waved her hand. "Bah. Let's get on with the smudging. Do you remember what all of this is?"

Mina toyed with digging into Lacey's reluctance to discuss her fireman. In the past, Lacey rarely gave in to Old Mina's badgering, and she couldn't afford to chase her sister off. Mina let it go. Granma had performed the ritual enough over the years, the cycle had burned into Mina's brain. *She knew I'd need it someday*. Sneaky. Yet Mina had never performed it herself. She pointed to a small bundle of dried branches and leaves tied with string, one end of which was charred. "White sage. We'll burn it and the smoke is supposed to clean the house of negative energy and set the spiritual tone."

"Nope." Lacey's earrings swung with the shake of her head. "You have to *know* it will banish the negative energy and set the tone. If you don't believe it in your heart, you might as well not do it at all."

Do or do not. There is no try. Words from a long-ago movie which had somehow stuck. She now believed she could see ghosts. She could believe the smoke would cleanse the house. "Let's do this."

"We'll start at the porch and work our way in through the house. You think you can do it on your own or do you want to watch?"

"I'll try it myself." She needed to learn to do it right. Jake deserved her best.

"You'll know if it works. No more Beedy in the house." She wrinkled her nose. "The guy always creeped me out. Felt like he was taking my clothes off while looking at me."

"If you think he was creepy in life, you can't imagine death." Mina shuddered. "Let's get this done."

She and Lacey worked their way through the first floor. Then the second, and the attic. Finally, the back porch. With each room, Mina would repeat the words Granma had said while ushering the purifying smoke to the corners. The certainty this would work grew with each room. When she finished, she ground the bundle into the abalone shell to extinguish the sage, then set it in the iridescent natural bowl.

"Good job." Lacey had trailed Mina, even up the rickety steps to the third floor. "I think I won't have to come out here to smudge anymore." She started to put the supplies back into the dining room's sideboard.

A loud muffler suddenly roared outside and Mina whipped a glance over her shoulder. Her gaze shot through the window.

A jacked-up truck slinked in front of the house, so slow it demanded notice. The widows had been tinted enough she could barely discern a human shape inside. A white square on the door proclaimed the owner.

Majors Construction.

As she tracked the vehicle's creeping progress past the house, shivers ran through Mina, raising the hair on the back of her neck to join the goosebumps.

"There's some serious negative energy." Lacey used opposing hands to rub at the goosebumps on her own arms. Her gaze grew distant as if staring into the depths of time. The same expression Granma used to have. A vision.

Mina flicked a gaze back to the street. Thank goodness it looked like Brian had left.

Lacey emerged from her momentary paralysis and set her fingers to massaging her temples. She'd said visions often gave her a headache. She didn't talk much about them. Because Mina hadn't believed in the Flannigan Gift or because Lacey didn't want to talk about it? Mina would have to explore that.

Lacey lifted her gaze. "Black is the answer."

Mina's goosebumps grew goosebumps of their own. "Black what? Brian's black pickup?"

Lacey shook her head, curls swinging around her shoulders. I don't know. "Black's all the Gift gave me. You'll have to figure out the rest."

TWENTY-TWO

"Come on Chief. Please?" Mina put every ounce of wile, guile, and personal history behind her plea. She'd waited until Garrett got home before she called and asked to meet Daniel. The lawman had looked like he'd been enjoying his time with the townsfolk at the picnic, but then, as with nearly about everyone else in the entire world, his social skills were better than Mina's.

The Chief swung his black, ostrich-quill boots up to the desk, reclined in his high-backed, padded leather chair. His large-knuckled hands folded over his stomach, only now as he approached sixty showing the effects of Clara's chicken fried steak. Behind him, the window let in the mid-afternoon light. "The only reason Clara's still here is the Rangers. They think the Eastland County Jail will be too intimidating. They'll transport her tomorrow, then she'll see the judge, then maybe get an attorney."

Days in jail? What would that do to the poor woman? "You know she didn't do it."

"I'd like to say I thought she wouldn't have been the one. She knew where the gun was, and what it looked like. Hard to argue with her confession."

She flopped back against the leather. "I don't believe it."

"Yet, there it is."

It couldn't have been her. *Time to use your head.* "What was the time of death?"

"M-E in Fort Worth said between six and ten p.m. Monday night."

One for their side. "She was working that evening, clocked out at nine-forty-five. Not much time to shoot him."

Daniel lifted a grizzled eyebrow as speculation filled his gaze. "Y'all don't open on Mondays."

"She was baking pies. Usually works Monday evenings to start the week. All of her pies were done and I have no reason to believe she padded her time."

"Okay." He seemed to accept her information. "But we don't know where he was shot. She said she shot him at her house, but we couldn't find any evidence there or in her car."

They must've searched her house. Poor Brittany and the kids. More drama. But at least they hadn't found anything. Point two. "Why'd she kill him?"

"She said he was lurking around in her yard and she shot him to defend herself."

Point three. Except... "Why didn't she call 911 if she thought it was someone on her property? She lives in the country. And no one would blame her for defending herself."

"She couldn't say why she didn't call."

What to ask next. Ah. "Where'd you find the gun?"

For a moment, she didn't think he'd answer, then he said, "At Brittany's house when we were gathering evidence. It was in a drawer, it matched the caliber and it had been fired recently."

Clara had sacrificed herself. No doubt existed in Mina's mind. "Does the gun match the bullet found in him?"

His eyes narrowed. "How'd you know they found one in him?"

"A guess." She smirked. "Does it match?"

He paused before saying, "We're still waiting on ballistics."

"Is it at least the right caliber?" She lifted a brow with the sarcasm.

"Yes." The word emerged with a rusty chuckle.

"A three-fifty-seven. Give us a little credit. We wouldn't have arrested her if it wasn't."

Shoot. "Were her fingerprints on it?"

His eyes narrowed. "That's not back yet, either."

Now she was baiting the bull. "Why would she put him in my shed? *How* would she put him in my shed?"

His boots hit the floor with a *thunk* and he leaned crossed forearms on the glassed top of the giant antique oak desk. "Any thoughts on heading to law school?"

Looks like interrogation time is over. She spread her hands. "Me? No. I just can't believe Clara would do it.

"*Humph.* Really? Why do you want to talk to her?"

He deserved the truth. "Because I want to find out why she's lying to you."

"Why does it matter? She claimed she shot him in self-defense. She'll be out of jail soon enough on bond with Beedy's reputation."

Mina tamped down her frustration. "She's a friend. And I think she's covering for someone."

Too-sharp eyes narrowed above his sun-leathered cheeks. "Do you have information you're holding from me?"

"No." She had to keep it to a word as guilt flooded

through her. But she still didn't think speculation enough to give to him as real information.

He studied her from under his bushy brows. "I'll allow it," he finally said.

"Why?" As soon as she'd uttered the word, she could've kicked herself for opening the door for him to renege.

His gaze slid away for a moment, then came back to her. "Because I've owed your Grandmother a favor for longer than you've been alive. She never called on it. I think now's the time for repayment."

A story hid behind those words, one he didn't seem to want to explain. She left it alone. Instead she said, "Thanks. Will it be recorded?"

"There aren't any recording devices in here." He flattened his hands and pushed up. "I'll be back in a couple of minutes." He exited a side door, one which led into the belly of the police department.

A great black pit grew in her gut as Daniel's words about law school came back to her. Who did she think she was taking on something like this? She owned a diner. *You're just another armchair investigator hyped up on too many true-crime shows thinking you can solve a mystery better than the cops.* Good gravy. It'd be a better idea to hock her monstrous Victorian for a good attorney to ensure Clara got a fair shake.

But you're a Flannigan. You have the Gift. And we don't back down.

She started, heart hammering, and looked over her shoulder. Where did that come from? And in Granma's voice no less?

The rattling of the door knob pulled Mina out of her thoughts, back to what she hoped to accomplish. Get Clara out of this and find the real killer.

The hallway door opened. Although he didn't make an appearance, Daniel's voice sounded. "Fifteen minutes."

Clara shuffled in and the thick, wood panel shut behind her. "What do you want?" The tone could best be called surly, something Mina had never heard from her friend before.

Oh boy. Clara may be sweet, but also stubborn. "I wanted to make sure you were alright."

"I'm fine." Clara didn't even glance her direction.

"Why don't you have a seat?" Mina patted the arm of the chair next to her and was mildly surprised when Clara took her up on the offer. "Do you need anything?"

She shook her head in the negative.

"An attorney?"

Another shake, this time staring out the window where sunshine played on the oaks' leaves in the square.

Most would take Clara's refusal to look at her as a measure of guilt. Not Mina. Clara didn't do this and didn't want Mina to interfere. Too late. Mina wouldn't let a friend rot in jail for doing something she hadn't done. "A good attorney will be able to poke so many holes in this case, all you'll have accomplished is denying yourself two years of income, and possibly lose the house you and Roger saved a long time to buy."

The comment earned her a glance. "What holes?"

A ha. A crack. "Let's start with the most obvious. You were working that night."

"The time of death could've been after I left." Clara's body, held stiff, looked as if it would snap at any moment, but she didn't budge.

"Not according to the Chief." Small lie, but she had to shake Clara up. *Time for the wild guess.* "Your fingerprints won't be anywhere on the gun, will they?"

Tears began to track down Clara's plump cheeks. She swiped at them with one hand, dragging along the other handcuffed to it. She lifted her chin. "I wore gloves."

The pieces had fallen into place. "When you think someone's creeping in your backyard?" Mina didn't wait for Clara to answer. "I'm betting someone else's fingerprints will be found on it. I'm betting you *think* it will be Brittany's and you're trying to save her from jail. Am I right?"

Her fingers laced together, gripping hard enough that her knuckles turned white.

Mina waited. It had worked a couple of times with Lacey, and if Lacey would crack under silence, maybe Clara would as well. Mina examined her friend during the lengthening pause. The curls Maisy set every other week for her at the *Hair Cuttery* were mussed and flatted in the back. Otherwise, in her own clothing of a floral patterned trapeze top, black crop pants, and orthopedic sandals, Clara could sub for Mrs. Claus on spring break, not a prisoner. Except for the handcuffs. Why hadn't they put her in a jumpsuit like the other prisoners Mina had seen in the past? Maybe they'd give her the prison orange at the county jail. Mina hoped it wouldn't get that far.

Clara said, "I didn't kill him." Her gaze remained fixed on the window and her voice came from miles away. "Brittany can't lose the children. The gun's registered to her and was in her house. It had been fired. She doesn't have an alibi for the time of Wayne's death. The kids were asleep." She turned to Mina, eyes feral. "She can't go to jail." Her lower lip trembled then her shoulders slumped. "I can't lose her. She's all I have left." Her head fell into her hands and great sobs wracked her body.

Mina jumped from her chair and threw her arms around the older woman's shoulders. Finding the murderer for Wayne didn't matter any longer. Her friend needed her. "I am going to figure out who killed Wayne. *I* don't believe it's Brittany. *You* don't believe it's Brittany. I understand you want her to be safe. If you think you can make it in Eastland County Jail until I can muddle through this, you need to get an attorney. The Rangers will be here tomorrow morning to interview you. Don't say anything to them. It'll delay things." Mina regarding Clara at arm's length. "Can you do that? Do you need money for a lawyer?"

Clara nodded. "I've got some savings," she said, each word drawn out as if through molasses in January.

"If you need it, I can help." Mina held up a hand when it appeared she'd get an argument. "Consider it a loan. We can work on terms later."

"Okay."

"Do you want me to call Larry Williams for you?" The local attorney wasn't Supreme Court material, but certainly competent enough to escort Clara through court.

Clara's mouth pursed but she nodded.

Relief surged through Mina. She couldn't stand the knowledge Clara would sacrifice herself when it was probably for nothing.

The knob rattled before the door swung open and Daniel appeared. "Time. She'll have to go now."

Mina could only nod. Her gaze flashed to her cook. "You'll be okay?"

Clara nodded slowly. "Thank you, Mina."

As the older woman shuffled back out, Mina could only be humbled by the gratitude in Clara's eyes. Mina prayed she was worth it.

Now it was time for Mina to get off her butt and get to business.

TWENTY-THREE

Later that evening, Mina set her wine glass on the granite counter and studied Olivia, who sat across the corner of her kitchen island studying Mina right back. Jake played in the Summers's backyard in the twilight with Olivia's children, George and Loretta. Mina had been too keyed up with her discoveries to wait for Garrett to get home from helping put in the security system in the Cup. Plus, the idea of keeping her reversal on the Flannigan Gift from her best friend rankled. Yet she bobbed and weaved, choosing small talk over what hovered in the back of her throat.

Olivia pursed her mouth and leveled Mina a gaze. "Spill it."

Mina blinked. Maybe Olivia was a little bit psychic? Ha. Probably just knew her life-long friend well enough to know she held something back. Yet Mina couldn't help but deflect. "Spill what?"

"Why you're here." She held up her index finger. "Exhibit one. You never have a glass of wine when Garrett's not here to drive." Another finger joined the first. "Two. You've been hitting me with nothing but small talk. You don't do idle chit chat. Three. Why make the trip out here unless it's big? You could've called. Four. You've nibbled your thumbnail to your first knuckle, which you only do when something's really bothering you, like when you and Garrett separated earlier this year." Her eyes grew wide with concern. "Oh, honey, you guys aren't getting a divorce, are you?"

"No!" Good gravy. "No, we're fine. It's not that." Thank goodness. She loved Garrett with all her heart. Just had a hard time showing it sometimes.

"Whew." Olivia wiped a dramatic hand across her forehead. "For a minute there, I thought you were going to tell me you and Garrett weren't going to work out."

Mina cheeks heated a bit with the memory of their reconciliation. Some things you couldn't share, even with your best friend. The embarrassment pushed the truth out of her mouth. "No. I see ghosts." Her lips slammed shut.

Olivia's hand stilled in its path to deliver a sip of wine. "I'm sorry?"

"I said I see ghosts," Mina mumbled into her wine glass. A healthier-than-normal swig of liquid courage caught in her windpipe and she coughed, spewing the pinot grigio across the shiny granite. "Oh, dang," she said through her fingers. She dashed for the paper towels, but Olivia waived her away.

"I've got it." She ripped a length and set to cleaning up while Mina washed her hands and dabbed a wet paper towel at the trails on her t-shirt.

Mina tossed the towel in the trash hidden by the simple, off-white cabinetry. "Great. Now I'm going to smell like a winery. I'm sure DDPD will pull me over on the way home and I'll be thrown in jail with Clara."

Olivia lifted her brow. "You said you see ghosts?"

Shoot. Mina needed to get better at deflection. She studied the toes of her tennis shoes. "Yes." Could her friend even hear her whispered confirmation? She'd pep-talked herself all the way over here and now what she'd feared her entire life might come to fruition. She couldn't stand it if Olivia ridiculed her. Olivia had been silent for long a long time and Mina glanced up and met speculation. "No. No. I don't. At all." She reached for her purse next to her on the counter. "I'm going to head out. Thanks for the wine and sorry for the mess."

"Wait, Mina." Olivia put a hand on her friend's arm. "I didn't know what to say." Encouragement curled the edges of Olivia's lips. "You have to admit, this isn't like you."

"I know. Nothing's 'like' me lately." Mina dropped her purse back on the counter, propped her elbows on the stone's surface, and hug her head in her hands.

"So, is this a Flannigan Gift thing, or something different?"

The gentle questioning brought Mina's head up, along with her heart. "I assume it's part the Flannigan Gift, but..." She managed to halt her words before she let it slip Jake could see spirits as well.

"But?"

"Nothing." Mina shook her head. "I wanted to tell you the other day in the shop, but, I chickened out."

Olivia hooted a laugh. "Mina Flannigan Shaffer chickening out? It's going on the calendar."

"Har, har." But better to be laughed at for being a coward than a crazy fool.

"Why tell me now?"

"Because you're my best friend, and I need a strategy session."

"For what?"

"Who really killed Wayne Beedy."

"Why in the world do you care who killed Wayne? As long as the police didn't think you did it?" She gasped and covered her mouth with her hand. "Tell me you're not a suspect."

Mina snorted a laugh. "No. I'm not officially a suspect. You know, I had a plan of how I was going to tell you. Let's start at the beginning." The whole tale tumbled out. Mina finally stumbled to stop with confronting Clara at the police department two hours ago.

Olivia hadn't said a word during Mina's recitation of the days since Mina had first seen Beedy's ghost. She had refilled her wine during a pause when Mina recalled her encounter with Stacey, but otherwise, Olivia's attention remained riveted on the story, eyes widening, frowning or laughing with the twists and turns. Now, she stared at her empty wine glass, sliding it back and forth across the counter with one hand—Olivia's thinking mode.

"You're sure it isn't Brittany?"

"That's your first comment? Nothing about Wayne's ghost?"

Olivia planted a hand on her jean's covered hip. "If there's one thing I know about you, it's you aren't a liar. If you say you see ghosts, that it's part of the

Flannigan Gift, then you do. What else is there to say?"

Mina dredged up a couple from her childhood. "Uh, you're a freak, Mina Shaffer. You're a crazy Flannigan girl, Mina Shaffer. Only whack-jobs talk to ghosts, Mina Shaffer. You know, the usual."

"I always did believe your Grandmother had the Sight. And Sunny found my grandmother's watch in an antique store in Abilene about two years ago." Olivia shrugged slim shoulders clad in an ancient Dew Drop Dragons t-shirt. "I'm a Flannigan Gift believer."

Mina gasped. Olivia, too? Did everyone believe in it but Mina? "Why didn't you tell me?"

"Because it would've aggravated you." Olivia deposited their wine glasses in the sink. "Since I'd known you in first grade, you've never believed. Why poke The Meanest Girl West of the Mississippi?" She delivered the jab with a raised brow.

"Yeah, well, now I have a murder to solve, and more than enough suspects to choose from."

Olivia winced a little. "I hate to even ask, but what does Garrett think about all this?"

"He thinks we should leave it to Chief Ruiz or the Rangers to solve."

"He's probably right."

Too much rode on this for Clara. "I know, but

Clara can't afford to be out of work for long. Brittany's still recuperating from her accident and she didn't have renter's insurance on Doc Bannister's house." It had been a tidbit gleaned from Clara yesterday. "So, I think we start with Stacey. Because I have an idea."

TWENTY-FOUR

Many of Dew Drop's businesses weren't open on Mondays, including the Cup. Counted in that number was Boyd's Fine Antiques. Luckily, both businesses shared a back alley, so it was a short, stealthy trip in the early morning light.

"This is the most illegal thing I've ever done." Olivia whispered from over Mina's shoulder as they stood at the back of Stacey's store.

"We're not here to steal anything or drink some beer at the river," Mina hissed back. "Just keep a lookout. We need to see if her gun is here or if there are any other clues."

Surprisingly, Mina found a regular round knob with an old inset key lock on the ancient wooden door. "Huh. You'd think she'd have better security than this." She twisted the handle. No dice. She wouldn't have been so lucky to find it unlocked. Both Mina and Olivia were uncomfortable with an actual break-in, so they hadn't brought any tools with them.

But if they could find something unlocked or at least loose, it wasn't a burglary, right? Besides, they could say they saw the open door or window and thought maybe Stacey had forgotten to shut it. Lord knows the wind from the southwest had been strong enough last night to push something open if it hadn't been latched. As long as neither of them cracked under scrutiny, they should be good.

Mina moved to the window next to the door, a small wooden double-hug. Its single-paned wavy glass spoke of being original to when the building had been constructed. It sat under five feet from the pavement. She could slide through if Olivia gave her a boost.

Left without an outside handle to grip, she put her palms on the ancient glass and pushed up gently. She caught her breath. The window wiggled more than it should.

Mina turned to her much taller friend. "Can you reach the upper part of the lower window's sash? It may be unlocked, but I'm afraid to push too hard on the pane." Lacey had a scar on her arm where she'd had to get twenty-two stitches after accidentally sliding into one of the Victorian's original windows as an eight-year old. The fragility of old glass and the damage it could do falling from its sash made Mina's stomach clench. There had been blood everywhere and it had ruined one of Granma's best cup towels. But if this window could be slid up...

Olivia put her fingertips on the thin sash and shoved it up enough to get her fingers under the frame, then gave one more push. "We're in." Olivia's conspiratorial wink belied her earlier trepidation.

"Boost me?"

Olivia bent at the knees and cupped her hands, like she had over a decade ago as a Dew Drop High cheerleader.

"I'm probably not as light as Ramona What's-Her-Name." Olivia's 'flyer' from the squad had Mina beaten in height by an inch, but they'd carried the same slim frame.

"I think I got it."

Mina put her foot in the cup, her hands on the window frame and on the count of three, up she rose, guiding her head through the opening then right on through to the floor. Which she hadn't counted on. "Oof." Her hands hit the wooden planks, but she allowed them to collapse, ducked her head, sucked in her gut to execute an awkward, but effective, somersault into an open area. No one screamed. She clambered to her feet. Light from the single window showed a storage area, one wall lined with bulky items covered in drop cloths. She held her breath, waiting for the blare of an alarm to announce to the world she'd just broken into a building. She glanced at the wall next to the door. No alarm panel.

Curious. Why wouldn't someone who keeps valuable antiques, like vintage MontBlanc pens and other easily stolen items, not have a security system? Meh. Why had she waited this long to put one in at the Cup? Maybe Stacey didn't think someone dared break into her store. She snorted a laugh at the idea as she brushed herself off.

"Hey!" Olivia whispered through the window.

"Wait a second." Mina checked her weird sense for detecting other people around her. She got Olivia by the whining in her ears, but nobody else increased the tone. She mentally crossed her fingers that this meant no one else was in the building. A quick turn of the knob and her friend scooted through.

"Aren't you going to close the door?" Olivia asked, her head on a swivel.

Mina used the inset brass pull to shut the window. "No. It was 'ajar'." She used air quotes around the word. "We came to inspect to make sure no one was inside, remember? Can you reach the thumb latch?"

"Oh. Right." Olivia nodded, then flipped the high window's latch with ease.

"I envy you."

Olivia smirked.

Mina crept toward the storage room's opening and found a hallway. No lights shone above or further down, just the glowing rectangle of light from the opening to the showroom. She turned to motion Olivia forward, but her friend had her back in the literal sense, barely a step separated them. Mina flipped on her phone's flashlight and shone it toward the floor to avoid alerting passers-by on the street. The short hallway had a bathroom on one side, and a closet with cleaning supplies on the other. Mina's heart sank. No office, which meant the only place to look for clues was the desk on the salesfloor with its expansive plate glass windows on either side of the door. Anyone passing by may be able to see them. Great. Go back or forward? They'd already entered. Nothing to be done but keep going. Clara was depending on her.

Thumping spy music in her head beat in time with her heart as she and Olivia moved from furniture vignette to vignette. She peered around a massive chest of drawers. Next stop, the desk, and if providence was merciful, Stacey's gun. She turned to

Olivia, who peered at her from the edge of an armoire off her left side. "Keep a look out."

"Got it." She popped up above the mattress of an ornate tester bed against one wall, then crouch-ran to a velvet sofa ahead of the desk Mina would search. The Victorian piece would provide excellent view of both the show windows and the back of the shop. Olivia flashed the thumbs up sign.

Bent almost double, Mina scurried to the desk. Here goes nothing. Four drawers, two on either side of where a person's legs would fit. The piece, with its slim curving legs and inlaid wood floral designs, had no pencil drawer or visible locks.

Tension formed a prickly ball in her stomach. Would someone leave something important in an unlocked drawer? This could be for nothing. *Should've thought of that before you burglarized Stacey's store, stupid girl.*

She picked the right side and slid open the top drawer. Pens, cheap ones compared to the one in its holder on the desktop, a stapler, and a mass of breeding paperclips cluttered the inside. Dang. Mina shut it and slid open the one below. Papers and receipts. Shoot. She almost closed the compartment, but something stilled her hand so she could thumb through the papers. At least half were bills and invoices for running the business, such as rent receipts, electricity, water and the like. The other half were written in Spanish from a company *Antiguedades Neuvos* at an address in Nuevo Laredo. Wasn't it across the border from El Paso? She hazarded 'New Antiques' from her rusty college Spanish.

Huh.

Invoices. If she had only kept up more with the language. 'S*ofa moreno.*' Easy enough. 'Purple sofa'. Mina's gaze flashed to the gorgeous antique Victorian couch with ornate wood carving spanning the back above lush purple velvet tufting. It took pride of place in the middle of the showroom.

On the next invoice she made out 'bed', '*cama,*' and somehow she remembered '*mesa de comedor y sillas de madera de roble*' meant 'dining table and chairs of wood of', though '*roble*' didn't translate. The order indicated one table, ten chairs and two '*sillones*' which was close enough for an armchair reference. In the back of the showroom, she and Olivia had passed a huge light oak table with massive carved legs and a set of twelve matching chairs, the two on the end with arms. She continued flipping through the sheets, somewhere around fifty, but no bill of sale for a handgun lay within. She moved to put the papers back, but she stopped. Could something be hidden in a false panel? She knocked on the bottom of the drawer, but no hollow sounded, only thin wood.

"Geezus," Olivia stage-whispered. Her hand pressed on her chest above her heart. "Warn me the next time. I dang near jumped out of my skin."

"Sorry." Mina slid the drawer closed, then moved to the other side of the chair. Of course it wouldn't be this easy. She slid the shallow left upper open to find tangled cords and several old mobile phones. Next, she slid out the deeper left lower drawer. Cosmetics—compacts, old lipstick and the like. To save Olivia's delicate nerves, Mina eyeballed the drawer bottom and all seemed real. *Gah*. Nothing. She slid it shut as well.

"Psst. Olivia, let's go." Mina started working her way to the back, where she met her friend.

"What did you find?"

Mina yanked at the door, which had mostly swung shut in their absence. "Later, let's get out of here and we'll call DDPD." The panel swung open and the black hole of a gun barrel met her gaze.

TWENTY-FIVE

"Mina?" The Chief dropped his hand and the gun hung at his side.

Mina's heart beat so hard, it felt as if it would gallop out of her chest. "Good gravy, Chief, don't scare me like that."

"Scare *you*? You almost got shot." Red replaced the pallor in his face. "Why are you two in here?"

"The door was wide open," Mina blurted. She looked at Olivia, who appeared relieved, possibly that Mina had taken the lead. Or it could be she didn't sport a massive bleeding hole in her stomach. "We weren't sure if someone broke in there or if she hadn't locked it and the wind blew it open."

"It was blowing so hard last night it rattled our windows," Olivia chimed in with a casual hand gesture. "I'm sure the wind pushed it open."

The Chief's scrutiny jumped from Mina to Olivia, then back again, his brows lowered above narrowed whiskey-brown eyes. He holstered the enormous black automatic pistol and snapped a strap down to hold it in place.

Mina's nerves began to skitter, but she managed to keep her mouth shut. If she and Olivia could brave this out, they'd be home free.

"No one was inside?" He crossed his arms over his chest and assessed them from the corner of his eyes.

"Nope." Mina shook her head for emphasis. Sweat began to roll down between her breasts. What would she tell Garrett if she had to call him from jail?

He let out an angry gust of air. "I guess it matches what Stacey said, then."

Instead of relief, the prickly ball of nerves doubled in size. "Stacey?"

"She called and said a couple of minutes ago her motion sensors were going off. I came over here immediately and found you two." He held up his other hand and spoke into a black hand-held radio. "Ruiz to Pinkerton. Come to the back." His tone sounded more like a bark.

The nerve ball rolled around, stabbing Mina with the urgency of how close they'd been to getting caught in the act, or worse, shot. Soon enough, sandy-haired Matt Pinkerton rounded the end of the line of stores and strode down the alley toward them.

The Chief explained what he'd found and Matt's gaze swung between his chief, Mina, and Olivia during the explanation. At the end, he hooked his thumbs on this thick belt. "You ladies could've been hurt if a burglar was in there. What were you thinking?"

"Thank you for putting it that way, Matt." Chief Ruiz glared at Mina. "I was mad enough, I didn't think I could get it out without shaking the both of you."

Mina's hands spread wide. "It's Dew Drop. What goes on here?"

"A murder." The men said the words in unison.

The Chief's index finger began to wag. "We've talked about this, Mina. Keep your doors locked and your security system working. Garrett did get both the house and the Cup done, right?"

"He's finishing up the Cup today. He ran into a couple of problems so we're bringing in an expert."

"Dang it, Mina. You know Brian Majors is still out there. You need to take care."

"He's no good," Matt added.

The nerve ball evaporated in the flash-heat of annoyance at all the lecturing. "Good grief. I'll get on

Garrett. But he's been busy figuring out the employee stealing from him."

"It's why we were in the area and could come fast, we were over at Shaffer's arresting Everly Beedy." Daniel said.

It couldn't be. "Everly?" Her mouth hung open for a second before she snapped it shut. "Why? Garrett thought the world of her. I did too. She never missed work. Garrett said she even asked for extra shifts, said she wouldn't take management pay if he could get her clerk shifts."

"She told Garrett Wayne never paid her the child support he owed and she couldn't make ends meet with her mother living with her. It's why she needed the extra shifts, but it still wasn't enough. She wanted it to be a loan, but couldn't pay it back." Chief Ruiz's mouth gained a sad twist. "Kinda felt bad for her. Lord knows, Wayne was as dead a deadbeat as ever walked."

Mina couldn't agree more. That man had much to answer for in the afterlife. Goosebumps rose and began to rampage across her skin. Everly. She had information about Wayne's death.

"Can I talk to her?" She blurted out.

"She's still in the back of my car," Matt said as his eyes slid to his boss.

Chief Ruiz's mouth tightened and he lasered his gaze on Mina. "I don't think it's a good idea."

"I just want to make sure she's okay. That her mother can watch after her kids." Good gravy. Where had she picked up lying like this? But the sense she must speak with Everly Beedy lay on her shoulders like a two-ton angus bull.

The Chief shifted his weight while he considered.

"Please?"

His mouth twisted. "Okay. You do realize your reputation as is going to get ruined if you continue to be nice to people like this."

"Thanks for the warning," Mina said dryly. "And thanks for letting me talk to her."

"I'm going to go to my shop and finish some new inventory if it's okay?" Olivia said. "Don't forget you owe me breakfast, Mina." Olivia walked the opposite direction toward the back of her store without gaining the permission she'd requested.

Mina followed Chief Ruiz and Matt around the end of the buildings all squished together like row houses on the square. In front of Larry Williams' office, Matt's police car, a large black and white SUV with the DDPD logo on the sides, sat cross-wise in the slanted parking spots, engine still running.

Matt and the Chief stopped at the corner, in the

shade of metal awning arching over the sidewalk on the square. "We'll stay here so we don't overhear something we shouldn't. She's been cooperative, but...," the Chief said.

Mina's heart filled with love for the older man. He had a reputation for being a hard-nosed police officer, but he had compassion many didn't see. She hadn't lied when she said she wanted to make sure the children were okay. She hadn't told him she needed to ask a couple more questions.

Matt held up his key fob and punched a button with is thumb. "Door's unlocked. She's in the backseat, passenger side. Don't get in and keep the door open."

"Thanks guys." Mina crossed the short distance and opened the back door, slipping between it and the SUV's frame.

If misery had a picture, it would surely be Everly. Hazel eyes rose to meet Mina's above blotchy, tear-streaked cheeks. "I'm so sorry," she whispered before Mina could say anything.

"I know." Dang it. Mina liked the woman, despite her ill-advised relationship with Wayne. "Your kids going to be okay with your mom?" Mina kept her voice low enough it wouldn't carry to the two policemen.

She nodded, lower lip trembling.

"You know Garrett's policy. Why?" Garrett didn't accept theft from the store and pressed charges if someone stole from Shaffer's, even employees.

Her mouth, which had been quivering with the effort to keep back tears, clamped into a line. She looked into her lap where her hands were cuffed. "It was that damn Wayne. He's crazy behind on child support. If he was still alive, he'd never in his life be caught up."

As dead a deadbeat for sure. "How deep are you?"

Everly didn't immediately answer. After several seconds, she said, "Two thousand." Everly flashed her eyes to Mina, then dropped them again.

Mina whistled low through her lips. "That much, huh?"

"I could've paid it all back if he'd just have gotten the money he said he was going to get." Her tone could've cut steel.

The goosebumps returned, running across Mina's skin with a vengeance. Another clue? "What money?"

Everly sighed, then leaned her head against the back of the seat, eyes closed, mouth pursed. "He called me from jail right before he escaped and said someone owed him fifty thousand dollars. Bastard said he'd pay me back. Then he went and got shot."

A hand landed on Mina's shoulder and she jumped.

"Time to go," Chief Ruiz said.

Everly focused her gaze on Mina. "Would you tell Garrett I'll pay him back?"

"I will, Everly. I will."

TWENTY-SIX

"Blackmail?" Olivia's eyebrows shot up. "I didn't think Wayne was that smart." She took plastic-wrapped garments from a box and hung them on a bar.

If only you knew. Mina pulled a sausage, cheese, and jalapeño kolache from the bag she'd brought from Kim's Donuts. She took a grateful bite. There hadn't been time for breakfast this morning before getting Jake to school and checking out Stacey's shop. Now, Mina sat at a worktable in the back of Cowboy Chic Boutique. Once she'd swallowed, she said "It's the only thing I can think of to get him killed."

"Not a drug dealer?" Olivia dusted her hands off. She pulled a sugar-glazed pecan roll from the bag and bit into it with orgasmic glee. "Gosh, these are good. But not good for my diet." She shot Mina a mock glare. "I hate you."

Mina laughed. She'd selected it for her friend knowing her preference. "It's small. You have to indulge every once in a while. But if you don't want it, I can take it back." Mina reached for the sweet pastry in Olivia's hand.

She shifted it to her other side, away from Mina's half-hearted swipe. "You'll lose a hand."

Mina lifted an eyebrow. No doubt who would win a scrap, but she'd let Olivia pretend she had skills. "I don't think a dope dealer killed Wayne." She nibbled on her lower lip, debating what she could tell her friend. Olivia wouldn't care one way or the other right? But she'd pretty much promised Laura she wouldn't reveal the information. Compromise. "I think he was blackmailing Brittany. I found a note when I went to her house to get the kids some clothes."

Olivia's gasp echoed in the back storeroom. "What in the world did Brittany do to get blackmailed?"

"I promised I wouldn't say." Close enough to the truth.

A coaxing smile curved her lips. "But you can tell me."

"I know, but I promised. I can say it was for ten thousand."

A little huff spoke of Olivia's frustration at not

knowing but she let it go. "Everly said Wayne was going to get fifty thousand, right?"

"Yeah. Which means he had another victim. And I'm thinking Stacey."

Olivia's mouth hung open. "No way."

"Hear me out. If what Lois said was true, she saw them arguing, then Stacey pulled a gun on him and said she'd kill him first. He said she'd regret it. Though there wasn't a gun in her store, I didn't tell you what I *did* find." Mina couldn't help but pause for dramatic effect by popping the last morsel of the bun-encased, savory-cheesy-goodness in her mouth.

Olivia swatted her friend's shoulder. "Don't keep me in suspense."

"Invoices from a furniture maker in Nuevo Laredo," Mina said once she'd swallowed. "I think her antiques aren't exactly antiques." Mina described her translations and how some of them matched pieces in the showroom.

"Ooh. That would be enough motive. She's proud of her store." Olivia smirked. "'Fine European Antiques' my patoot." She finished the last of her pecan roll with a satisfied smile.

"And he'd think she had the money or she could get it from OP."

Olivia's index finger tapped her cheek while she chewed then swallowed. "I like it. It would make at least two blackmail victims as suspects. Don't you think it's time to tell Chief Ruiz what you found? Maybe Clara would be released."

"And tell him while we were in Stacey's store, supposedly looking for someone who broke in, we rooted around in her desk drawers? And I promised I wouldn't reveal Brittany's secret."

"Well, dang. I hadn't thought about it like that." She licked her fingers of the sugar glaze with a sigh, then her eyes darted to the bag.

"Yes, there's a second one in there," Mina said with a laugh.

"Arrgh!" Olivia reached in. "You are so bad for my diet," she mumbled through a mouthful of the second pecan roll.

"My diet, too," Mina said, if just in solidarity. She finished her second kolache as Olivia demolished hers. Mina wadded up the bag and tossed it in the trash can. "I guess there's nothing to do now. I can't tell the Chief what I know and I don't really have any proof anyway, other than a bunch of gossip." She sighed. "I guess I'll go get my truck an oil change before I deliver the pies to the church board retreat."

Truck. Why did it stick in her head? The truck tire mark in the alley behind her house. A glint of silver flashed in her mind.

OP's new truck.

"I thought of something." Mina said slowly.

Olivia paused slitting open the next box with a cutting blade. "What?"

Pieces started sliding into place. "OP showed up the day after Wayne's murder in a beater ranch truck, not his black Ford. The day after, he had a brand new truck."

Olivia tapped her toe, eyes staring into the distance as she considered Mina's words. "You're implying OP or Stacey killed Wayne and used his truck to dump his body, then they got rid of the truck to ditch the evidence?"

Mina nodded.

Olivia scrunched her brow and remained silent for several seconds. Finally, she brightened "It meets the timeline. She says she and OP are each other's alibi. It's not like OP isn't a Texan. Everyone knows he carries a gun with him everywhere. Has a concealed license for it."

Mina's adrenaline jumped. "What does he carry?"

"Shoot. I don't know. Waylon might. Hold on." Olivia pulled her phone from her purse, tapped on the screen, then held it to her ear. Her head tipped from side to side as she waited, then she smiled. "Hey baby, I can't tell you why I need it, but what caliber is the gun OP usually carries around?" She paused

GHOSTS, PIES, & ALIBIS   193

with pursed lips. "I see. Thanks baby, I'll see you at dinner tonight." She put her phone back in her giant, tasseled leather bag.

"Stop teasing me."

A sly smile slid across her face. "A three-fifty-seven."

"Good gravy. OP or Stacey could be the killer."

"But how could you prove it? We can't say we broke into Stacey's store to find the motive."

Around and around Olivia's question tumbled in Mina's mind. "Dang it. If I could only find the truck. Maybe there's a clue inside. Like blood or something."

"OP only buys his trucks at Harmon's in Eastland. You could try calling them. Maybe he traded it in thinking no one would ask about him replacing one only a year old."

"Good call." She high-fived Olivia, brimming with an energy which made her want to do zoomies, like Olivia's border collie. "I've got to get the pies to the First Baptist Church Board Retreat. Then I'll call and see if Harmon's has OP's truck. It may have been detailed already, but you never know."

"Make sure you call Garrett before you do."

The comment sucked all of the breeze from Mina's windmill. "Are you going to tell Waylon about this morning?"

"Heck, no." Olivia's expression screwed up in horror comical enough to send Mina into peals of laughter.

"Going to a car lot isn't going to be anything dangerous. I'll tell him afterward."

After all, what could go wrong?

TWENTY-SEVEN

Mina pulled a cool-carrier laden with four pies from the back seat of her truck. Two more made up the dozen ordered for the church's board retreat.

Behind her and across the recently expanded church parking lot, kids whooped and hollered on the elementary school playground. She'd scanned for Jake but it was an older grade. She hurried toward the church's administration office located in the two-story brick structure added on last year to the original sanctuary built with cattle money at the turn of the century. Once inside, blessed coolness replaced the overwhelming heat of a late summer which surely had to break soon.

"Hello?" Though plenty of cars were parked in the lot and the lights were on, none of the desks or offices were occupied. Not the secretary's, not the

Pastor's or the Associate Pastor's, Youth Pastor's or the Deacon's. *They must be in one of the meeting rooms.* She put the cool case on Lois's spotless desk and went back out to her truck for the remaining coolers.

When she returned, she fished the invoice from her back pocket. For some reason, Pastor Davis preferred to do everything in hard copy, rather than email. Whatever. As long as they paid, she didn't care. She laid the bill Lois's desk. Shoot. She'd forgotten the total at the bottom. A quick tabulation with her phone and she had the figure. She swiped a pen from atop a telephone message pad and started to fill in the digits, but the ink wouldn't flow. Gah. Lois didn't keep the cup of pens most secretaries usually kept brimming. Just the pad, telephone, a vase with fresh flowers probably culled from the Sunday altar arrangements, and a Bible Verse-A-Day calendar. *Well, whaddaya know.* Today's was Proverbs 10:18. Mina snickered.

Since it would be easier, not to mention cooler, to find a pen in Lois's desk rather than searching her truck, she crossed to the other side and opened the lap drawer. At first it was just a fraction to grab a pen in the well typically lining the front, but then she slid it further. Empty. Well, except for a couple of paperclips and a box of staples. Weird. Mina pulled at the top of the three drawers to the right. It contained only a manual for the telephone. The middle drawer didn't have any pens. Good gravy. She pulled at the bottom, its size said a file drawer, but maybe... She pulled anyway. It gave a little resistance, but then popped free with a tug. Inside, a couple of hanging files. Dang it. She'd have to go outside and dig through her truck console.

Her hand pushed to close it when a small, rectangular box in the back shadows caught her attention. A pen's box? Her phone rang and she looked at the screen. Garrett.

"Hey, you. What's up?" Guilt niggled at her about breaking into Stacey's store. Then Mina reminded herself the woman's attempted to seduce Garrett. The guilt melted away.

"I figured out who was stealing. Everly. It could only have been the managers, and I interviewed all three. Everly didn't last a minute before breaking down." He huffed a frustrated breath laced with disappointment.

"I talked her in the back of Matt Pinkerton's police car." She cracked the lid on the old box. A black pen with a gold clip and banding clattered onto the desk. Dang. She'd opened it upside down.

"You talked to her?"

She snagged the sleek plastic and pulled the cap.

Great. A fountain pen. Hopefully it had ink. "I wanted to make sure her kids were okay. She said something weird." The ink flowed and she filled in the total on the invoice. Nice pen. Heavy.

"Weird about her kids?"

"Not the kids." Mina put the cap back on the pen and set it on the box's velvet lining. She dropped her voice to a whisper. "She said Wayne expected a big payout from someone. Fifty thousand dollars. I think Wayne was blackmailing someone other than Brittany. She wouldn't have that kind of money."

"Really? Who?"

A rustling behind her made her whip around.

Lois stood ten feet behind Mina, eyes narrowed. Her expression smoothed out so quickly Mina almost thought she'd imagined the venom in the woman's glance. Probably a holdover from the gossip session Mina had overheard. She'd been disliked for the majority of her life, even if much of it was of her own making. The prospect of Lois not being her friend had little impact.

Mina shot a half-smile to the secretary. "Hey, I've got to go, sweetheart. I'm going to get the oil changed, then I'm running to Eastland for an errand."

"Shoot. Can you put those off until later? Steve was supposed to come by the Cup around one to finish on the security system. I'm stuck here since

Everly is not available and Dad had to make a run to Fort Worth. I can get Jake. What's up in Eastland?"

"Too long a story. I'll tell you when I get home." No time to put her suspicions about OP and Stacey on blast to Lois. "We need the security system finished, dang it. I'll be at the Cup by one, then. Love you." She put her phone in her back pocket. "Apologies. Here's the invoice for the pies." She handed the slip of paper to Lois with a smile bigger than West Texas.

Lois came forward to accept the invoice, face a tight mask of civility. "You can take them to the kitchen refrigerators." She stepped forward to the desk and Mina sidestepped to grab carry straps on the bags in both hands. Lois closed the bottom drawer, locked it with a key from a ring she fished from her denim skirt's pocket. She twitched the calendar a fraction then surveyed the perfectly neat surface with arms crossed at her chest.

Ah ha. A neat desk freak. "If you'd grab the other the cool bag, I can make one trip," Mina said.

A muscle flexed in Lois's cheek, yet she pasted as fake a smile on her lips as had Mina. "Sure."

Two sets of pies in Mina's hands, one Lois's, they made the quick trek to the congregation hall's kitchen in silence. "Lot of pies for the Board retreat," Mina said.

One slim dark brow rose, annoyance flashing in her expression. "We're treating the Board and their spouses to a dinner. Manly's Barbecue is catering," she said, tone crossing the line into snappish. "Board members do enough for the ministry and community in their spare time and away from their families. I don't think anyone would mind spending on pies."

Defensive a little? What's up with that? "Oh, a dinner? I thought they would be used over the week. I'm glad the families were included."

The wind seemed to fall from Lois's sails. "Well, then I can see we're in agreement. I need to get back." She pivoted abruptly on her heel and strode away without another word.

Wow. Mina shook her head at the woman's mercurial temper. She'd never seen this side of Lois. Maybe Mina shouldn't have gone through her desk? Then again, it could've been merely a bad day. Lord knows Mina had enough of them herself.

TWENTY-EIGHT

"Thanks for all of your help, Steve." Mina held the back door open for the technician.

"You bet." He touched where his brim would've been if his ball cap hadn't been on backward, then set down the spools of wire and his toolbelt a couple feet inside. He nodded to the box inset into the wall next to the door. "Garrett and I got a lot of work done last night, so I'm guessing it shouldn't take more than a couple of hours. Mostly an hour of wiring and then testing and tweaking the system."

"Great." Mina left him to finish whatever he had to do to defend the Cup against acts like what Brian Majors did to Brittany's home. This would be a good time to wash her windows, though the heat made it less than appealing. Maybe she could still get to Eastland today. She pulled out her phone and found the number for Harmon's. Steve didn't need to overhear, so she wandered away from his work area and made the connection.

"Thank you for calling Harmon, West Texas's Truck Headquarters. This is Greg."

"I needed to speak to someone about buying a new pickup. I'm looking for something specific."

"I'm a salesman. What are you looking for?"

"A friend, OP Boyd, traded in his truck last week." Mina winced a bit at using the term 'friend', but it worked with her narrative. "It was pretty new. I thought maybe I could look at it." She described the hulking vehicle.

Fingers tapping on keys sounded in the background. "I think we've still got it. A black Ford extended cab, extended bed?"

A little thrill shot through her. "That's it. Can I come check it out in a couple of hours?"

"Sure. We're open until seven tonight and I'll be here."

She ended the call, so much excitement rushing through her she could barely keep her feet on the floor. If this truck had a shred of evidence in it, she'd go to Chief Ruiz. She'd figure out a way to get around her little burglary. Heart light with the idea she may be able to solve the murder and get Clara out of jail, she stepped onto the sidewalk in front of the Cup with bucket, squeegee, and towel in hand. At least the bright turquoise and red metal awnings shaded enough of the sidewalk that she wouldn't melt.

Make it completely melt. Mina wiped her brow and fanned herself with her shirt. She'd only completed the two large side windows, and already sweat soaked her bra through. Dang. She'd only worn it once. And four more windows on the front to go. Prickles slithered up her spine as she bent over to pick up the bucket. She looked up to the street.

A black pickup slid slowly past her and she jolted with recognition. Through the dark tinted windows, Brian Majors stared at her, face screwed up in a twisted mass of hate.

She shivered. If looks could kill she'd be a dark spot on the sidewalk. She did a double take as it traveled away from the downtown. No decal this time on the door. And a license plate frame sat lopsided on one screw, obscuring the numbers and letters. The pickup roared off with a black puff from the diesel engine's tailpipe.

The bucket handle fell from her slack fingers. She fished the phone from her back pocket and found Chief Ruiz's contact.

"Mina?"

"Hey Chief. Brian Majors just drove by me slowly in front of the Cup. He didn't do anything, but it kind of freaked me out."

"Brian? In front of the Cup?" He swore a string blue enough to cause a seasoned cowhand to blush, unusual for him, at least in front of Mina. "Which way was he headed?"

A siren started wailing in the distance. "Out of downtown toward Sixteen."

"Thanks. And be careful. The Palo Pinto Sheriff found the school video showing him cutting Brittany's brake lines. They got a warrant and we've been looking for him since I saw you this morning. Even went by Fellowship Church where he was doing some maintenance. He's been as slippery as a greased pig."

The church must've wanted the lowest bidder. But *Brian Majors*? After he'd done so much damage to Brittany's house? As he'd mentioned it often, "I should have the security system finished today."

"Good. Call me if you see him again." The call cut off without a goodbye.

She shoved the phone back in her pocket, trying to shake off the heavy cloud pressing in on her. He hadn't done anything. *Yet*. She took a sip of sweet tea from an insulated cup. Even its lovely coolness couldn't wash away the lump of dread parked in her throat. Her gaze strayed to the camera Garrett and Steve had put up last night. Its field of view should catch anyone coming in the door as well as the cash register. The lump started to dissipate with the greater sense of security. She shook her head to rid herself of the last of the unease. These windows wouldn't clean themselves and it wasn't getting any cooler.

A 'sweaty mess' failed to describe her by the time she finished the windows. Through the sparkling-clean glass, Steve seemed to be wrapping up earlier than she thought. She flipped her wrist and her activity tracker said half past two. No time for a shower if she wanted to get to Eastland and back and still get dinner ready. She could clean up while the King Ranch casserole baked in the oven. Garrett's dad was coming over at seven, since Irene was at the board meeting. He didn't like many of the board members, including the new pastor, so it wasn't a wonder he didn't go to the dinner. She grimaced. Hopefully she wouldn't start stinking during the forty-minute trip to Harmon's. Maybe a quick cleanup in the Cup's bathroom would do the trick.

Steve filled the next half hour downloading the monitoring app to her phone and showing her the settings. She locked up the back door and pulled out with a toot of her horn while Steve continued to load his truck. So excited with this lead, she could barely restrain her speed.

Fastest way to Eastland followed Interstate 20. She turned her wheels north, air-conditioning running at full blast to finish what the Cup's cool air hadn't. In ten minutes, she crested big the hill leading down to the highway. She pushed the brake to slow down. Under her foot, the pedal bucked then went to the floor, all resistance gone. A lighted phrase flashed on her dash—'BRAKE FLUID PRESSURE LOW'. Mina pushed her foot again then again as her pickup traveled down the hill, gathering speed all the while. Panic coursed through her. *Shoot. Shoot. Shoot. What should I...?* Lower gear. She pushed the gearshift to '3' then down one more gear. With each bump the engine whined at a higher pitch, making her cringe, but she hadn't slowed hardly at all. She looked up to the intersection looming a couple hundred yards ahead. What now? She searched the interior and her eyes fell to her left, on the emergency brake's pedal. Yes!

She used her left foot to push down hard on the lever. Grinding sounds came from the engine compartment, but she couldn't worry about it now.

She was slowing, but not fast enough to avoid the tractor-trailer waiting to turn at the four-way stop.

Mina laid on the horn and rotated the dial for her lights. The eighteen-wheeler had the right of way.

There was no way she'd be able to halt at the stop sign.

TWENTY-NINE

Mina held her breath as her pickup sailed through the crossroads. Somehow, truckdriver interpreted her distress signals. But she wasn't out of the woods yet. Not until she stopped. The road leveled out ahead of her and she began to decelerate. She pulled off onto the narrow shoulder when she felt safe enough. The gravel helped slow the truck even more.

When she came to a complete halt, it took a second to register. She peeled her hands from the wheel. Looked down at herself to make sure she still lived. She giggled, then slapped a hand over her mouth before the laughter grew. *Whew. What a crazy ride.* Thank goodness the eighteen-wheeler driver didn't pull out in front of her. She said a quick prayer of thanks for Mr. Reese, her driving instructor. At sixteen, she'd laughed at the thought she'd need to know how to stop a car when its brakes failed. The old man told her she'd be surprised. An understatement. Terrified and panicked were more like it.

She'd need to call Garrett. She reached for her phone on the console.

"Hey babe." His voice held a note of affection she'd remember for the rest of her life.

"Hey, um I need..." Her voice faltered. "I—I..." The phone slipped from her nerveless fingers and bounced to the floorboard. The shaking started deep inside, worked its way to her limbs. Goosebumps broke out across her body. She wrapped her arms around her middle. *Hold it together.* She gasped for air while her heart pounded in her ears.

She huddled in a ball until the shudders finally receded and she gained control again over her breathing. She sought out her phone, eventually finding it under the seat. It buzzed in her hand and Garrett's handsome face showed on the screen.

"Are you okay?" He hadn't even waited for her to say a word.

She cleared her throat. "Yes. The brakes failed on the hill before the interstate and if it had been any later, I may have hit a truck." Her voice disappeared to a whisper.

"Where are you now?" All affection had disappeared, replaced by urgency.

"Still on Sixteen about a mile north of the intersection."

"I'll be right there. I love you."

"I love you, too." How close she'd come to losing him became all the more apparent. Her need for control and hatred toward herself could've driven away such a wonderful man, yet they'd survived their separation. It made her want to bang her head against a block wall that she could be that stupid.

A siren cried in the distance. An SUV rolled up behind her in short order. The door flew open and Chief Ruiz jogged up to where she'd rolled her window down. He leaned his forearms on what had to be blazing hot metal. "Garrett called. He's on his way. You okay?" Concern lined his features.

She laughed, dismayed she could still detect a wobble. "I would've gotten out, but I'm not too sure about my legs holding me up."

The Chief nodded his head. "You must've had an adrenaline dump. The shaky feeling typically doesn't last more than an hour. You want me to sit in there with you 'til Garret gets here?"

Tears threatened, but she pushed them back. "Yeah." She rolled up her window as he crossed in front of the vehicle.

"What happened?" he asked once he'd shut the door.

She described the events, finishing with a smothered laugh. "I have no idea how I remembered what Mr. Reese said to do."

He patted her hand where it rested on the console. "More important is a level head. I'm sure some of it was Mr. Reese's words, but you probably could recall them because you didn't panic."

"Crazy for my brakes to fail like that."

Daniel's face grew grim. "Yep."

She tensed. "You don't think Brian..."

"I don't know, but I'm going to find out." She'd never heard his voice carry so much determination. "Eastland County picked him up just before Garrett called me."

"Thank God." A knock on her window made Mina's head swivel to the sound.

Garrett. Oh, God. Garrett.

He pulled the door open and she fell into his arms. The tears she'd pushed away flowed freely now, and she hugged his waist with all her strength. Strong arms hugged her back, murmuring into her hair. She hiccupped to stop, wiping her cheeks with both hands.

"I'll stay with the car," Chief said over her shoulder. "You take her home."

"Thanks Chief." Her smile could only be what someone might call watery. "Don't worry. I won't tell anyone you're really a nice guy and ruin your rep."

Her attempt at humor drew a tender smile from him. "You're a champ. Now get on, you two."

During the ride home, she and Garrett held hands, even when they picked up Jake from school, but Mina didn't feel like talking. She was still consumed by the idea she almost lost this—her life with this wonderful man, wonderful son, wonderful friends. Tears threatened again and she sniffed them back.

Garett put the car in park when he pulled into the driveway. "I can tell Dad to grab dinner at Manly's if you want a quiet night."

"No, I enjoy Robert's company." She reached into the back seat for Jake's hand. It slipped into hers as he met her eyes. "I love you all. I want to be surrounded by it tonight."

She walked through the house, a new appreciation for every knick-knack, each piece of furniture, both those pieces she and Garrett bought together and those handed down through the generations. She stopped at her grandmother's favorite chair. Imagined the tiny woman with her silver hair and sharp, perceptive eyes. Her laugh and the tone she used when Mina had been especially mean to someone, leaving Mina devastated and certain she'd do better. She could almost see the woman who raised three young, parentless girls sitting in the wingback reading a book, trusty cup of tea next to her on the marble-topped Eastlake table.

The casserole she'd slid into the oven was hot and bubbly by the time Mina came down from her hot water tank-draining shower. She put the dish on a trivet to cool a bit. All King Ranch devotees knew eating it immediately from the oven would be taste-bud suicide. A quick salad in a large bowl and dinner was ready. Good thing, too. She needed a quiet night with the people she loved, but she couldn't have managed a whole meal from scratch.

Robert strode through the doorway, arms wide. "How's my favorite daughter-in-law after her near-death experience?"

"Ha, ha." She returned his hug. "Your only daughter-in-law is fine, and even more thankful for the wonderful people in her life."

"I always knew you were a smart woman. But then you married Garrett, didn't you?" He winked.

"I would every day, all over again." She handed him the salad and followed him into the dining room with the casserole, then called for Garrett and Jake.

Steaming plates of cheese and chicken and tomato and chilies didn't last long. Both Robert and Garrett had second helpings. She didn't talk much, soaking in the good-natured byplay between the three males at the table. Finally, both men slid their plates back with nearly identical happy sighs.

Mina picked up the casserole dish, one third of the King Ranch still remaining. "Isn't the church board meeting for the week? You want me to box you up some to take home for lunch or dinner since Irene won't be home?"

"I'd love it." A strange look flitted across his face and his eyes grew distant.

"What's up, Dad?" Garrett halted on his way to the kitchen.

"Nothing." Robert grimaced. "Well, something, really. Irene said several high-dollar items from the auction went missing between the tables and checkout. Three items, worth about two thousand dollars. Now we're going to have to figure out how to make it up in donations." He rubbed his eyes with his fingers and thumb. "I know we have almost a whole year until the next mission trip, but for our small community, it's a lot."

With the Cup closed today, Mina hadn't the benefit of the gossip train. Nosey must be going bonkers. "Wow. I hadn't heard anything went missing."

"That's just the thing. Pastor Davis doesn't want anyone to know about it and said they could've accidentally been misplaced. Thinks it would be bad for the congregation to believe they had a thief in their midst." He slapped his hand on the flat of the mahogany table making the silverware jangle against his plate. "They *do* have a thief and someone should find out who it is. But Irene says the Pastor also said it's not *Christian*. Baloney. It's not Christian to steal." Mina hadn't seen Robert worked up like this in some time, maybe ever. Usually he was as even-tempered as Bevo, the University of Texas longhorn mascot.

"What got stolen?" Hadn't the Chief said Brian was working there? Mina wouldn't put it past him for sure, especially if he had a drug habit.

"Irene wouldn't tell me. She said I got too worked up and she was afraid I'd go make a report to Daniel." He barked a laugh. "I probably would, too. Made me darn mad someone would not only take from kids, but take from kids who are going to be helping other people."

Garrett shook his head. "Practically half the town attended the picnic. Even the Chief. They stole those things from right out under his nose."

Then Brian was out. He wasn't part of the congregation and she hadn't seen him there that day. A strange, high-pitched beeping noise came from the kitchen.

Garrett winced. "What's that God-awful sound?"

It took a half a second to recognize it, then Mina scooted her chair back. "My phone. It sounds like the app Steven put on it for the Cup's security system." She hurried to the next room then returned, gazing at the screen. Then she looked up at Garrett. "This says there's been movement in the kitchen and dining area."

THIRTY

Garrett pulled is phone from the breast pocket of his Shaffer Hardware logoed button-down. "I'll call Chief Ruiz."

"Don't. Brian's back in jail." Her word stopped Garrett in the middle of dialing. "Steve said false alarms were pretty common early on until we got the motion sensors set properly to take in traffic on the sidewalk and the street." She tapped her code into the phone's keypad. "I've reset it, but I'll go down there to check there isn't a door open or something." Her visit to Stacy's shop earlier squatted in her mind. *Dumbest idea ever. Never again.* Ha. Like she'd ever be trying to find a murderer again.

Garrett put his phone back in his pocket and his napkin on the table. "I'll do it."

"Like it'd be any safer with *you* going down there

alone." She propped a hand on her hip. "Don't be silly. It's probably just a false alarm. Besides, Jake needs help with his homework. Math's still up for tonight and you explain it so much better than I do." She stuck out her tongue as if gagging.

"I'll go with her," Robert said. "I've heard that new math stuff is a bugabear."

Garrett's brows snapped together. "I don't like it."

"I promise to be careful, and with two people, no one's likely to try anything." She turned to her father-in-law, hopeful he'd continue to side with her. "Right?"

"I'm sure it will be fine. I'll make sure she doesn't go charging in if a door's open," Robert said with a wink.

Garrett's mouth twisted as if his tea had too much lemon. "Okay. But if you see anything suspicious, promise you'll call Chief Ruiz."

"Promise." She drew a big 'X' across her chest with a sassy smile, then held out her hand. "Can I borrow your truck?"

He fished his keys from the pocket of his jeans, put them in her palm with his over it and tugged her to him. His arms wrapped around her and leaned down to her ear. "Be careful. I almost lost you." His gruff tone meant the world to Mina.

She whispered back, "I will. Promise." With an extra hard squeeze, he let her go.

In five minutes, Mina pulled Garret's pickup into one of the slanted spaces in front of the Cup, but with her recent brush with danger, she waited until her father-in-law pulled in next to her to hop out. She stepped up to the glass door and tugged. Locked. In the late summer evening light, everything seemed to be in order, including the cash register. She didn't keep money in it when the café was closed, anyway.

"You want to follow me around to the back door to make sure?"

He shot her a deadpan look. "Garrett would have my butt if I didn't."

Around back, Mina tested the door and found it secure as well. "Thanks for coming with me," she said to Robert. "Oh, shoot. We forgot the casserole. Do you want to come back for it?"

"I'll be at the hardware store tomorrow to help Garrett. Have him bring it with him. I'll never turn down King Ranch casserole. Especially yours." He winked, then climbed into his truck and waited while she did the same.

With the parking in the back, it would be easier for him to back out first, which he did, then proceeded down the alley. Mina's phone rang as she reached for the gear shift. Chief Ruiz flashed in the caller ID, a number she wouldn't ignore.

"Mina," he said to her greeting. "How are you?"

"Fine." A little ball of tension settled onto her shoulders. "You calling to just check up on me?"

"Yes." A little pause grew then he said, "But also to let you know I had your car towed to Moe's. Your brakes were cut."

She shivered, recalling the slow drive-by earlier in the afternoon and the malice in Brian's sneer. "So he cut my brakes, too? Geez, I've never even met the guy." Yet his effect on her life had been enormous.

"He says he didn't. Hell. He says he didn't cut Brittany's either, but it's plain as day. He was stupid enough to drive his truck with the placard on it and they got it on the school's surveillance camera."

"Oh wow." Her shock turned to excitement as her eyes flashed up to the corner of the building. Maybe they'd caught him on camera. "Steve finished up over here this afternoon putting in the security system when Brian drove by. We've got a camera on the back door where I parked. Maybe we caught it on tape when Brian was messing with my truck. I'll look at the video."

"Don't worry about it tonight. I've got paperwork to finish up. I'll be over tomorrow to take a look at the footage."

"Sure. I'm leaving the Cup now. Call ahead and I'll have your chicken fried steak ready when you walk through the door."

He laughed. "You know I will."

She put the phone on the console and reached for the gear shift. Time to go home.

"You haven't done what you said you would."

Mina squealed and spun in her seat to find Wayne next to her in the cab. "Geez, you are always sneaking up on me. Where have you been? I haven't seen you in days."

"I can't be here all the time, and you don't exactly stick around one place now, do you. And since I can't come inside your house anymore, you've been harder to find. Did you figure out who killed me?"

Anger, hot and thick boiled over. "Oh, I found a lot. Like how you were blackmailing people." His quick shocked expression before it turned to innocence confirmed her suspicion. "Brittany and Laura. Stacey." She shook her head in mock dismay. "Good gravy, Wayne, it's no wonder you ended up dead. Which of those killed you?"

"It wasn't them. They paid me."

Hard metallic rap on her window caught Mina's attention.

A very large, black pistol loomed in her vision. Holding it was Lois Dearborn.

THIRTY-ONE

Lois shifted more into Mina's line of vision, large gun not wavering. She had on a dark hoodie with jeans, and kept her shoulders hunched, head lowered a bit. Mina's stomach bottomed out. It might be enough that someone wouldn't be able to distinguish who it was on the security camera in the evening light.

"Get out," Lois ordered.

Mina more read Lois's petal-pink lips than heard what she said over the heavy hum of the truck's diesel engine. For a brief moment, Mina considered throwing it into reverse and flooring it, but Lois would probably get a shot off before she could get anywhere. *This is Wayne's killer?* Mina got out of the truck and slammed the door. She held her hands up because, well, it's what you did when someone pointed what looked to be a .357-caliber weapon in your direction and you had nothing but your wits with which to fight back.

"Turn it off, you dumb witch," she said, her tone low and vicious. She motioned with the gun for extra emphasis.

Wayne appeared next to Lois. "It was her." His tone carried a sense of wonder. "Her." Angrier this time. He punched at Lois's midsection, but his fist and half of his forearm went right through.

Lois sucked in a breath with a grimace then looked around wildly, gun following her gaze before she turned back to Mina. Lois shoved the weapon toward Mina. "I said turn it *off*."

Mina lifted the door handle, but it didn't budge. *Crap.* "I locked the keys in the truck."

The other woman swore a string no godly church secretary should know. "Do you have the keys for the diner?" She clenched her teeth when Wayne tried to grab the gun. Her long, perfectly manicured finger tightened on the trigger.

Mina weighed the idea of lying. D*on't make her shoot you in the alley.* The longer she lived, the more chance she had of making it out of this alive. "They're in my pocket."

"Well get them out." Lois rolled her eyes. "Jesus. Do I have to tell you everything?" She motioned Mina toward the door with the gun.

Why would a church secretary kill Wayne? Visions of their interactions swirled around in Mina's head. Lois's exchanging unsavory gossip with Nosey, but what could've been in that conversation? Mina inserted the key in the lock. Wait. But Lois *was* one of the people in charge of the church's Youth Mission Trip fundraiser. She'd hovered over the tables during the picnic.

Mina pushed the door open and Lois's hand connected with Mina's shoulder, propelling Mina forward into the gloom of the short hallway. She couldn't regain her balance and ended up on the floor with a cry, momentarily stunned. The *thunk* of the deadbolt behind her made her scramble to her feet, backing up toward the kitchen to try to get distance between them. She might find a weapon. Against a gun? Maybe, but better get the other woman talking. "Why are you doing this?"

Lois kept pace with her the entire way on stealthy, black-sneakered feet. "If you had kept your hands to yourself and not gone nosing through people's personal stuff we wouldn't be here."

Mina's thoughts swirled like a dust devil. Personal stuff? When did she go through someone's personal stuff? Stacey's shop? What could Lois have to do with buying fake antiques? Stall. "I didn't mean any harm by it."

The other woman's eyes snagged on the glowing security system panel on the wall. "What's your code."

Mina had asked Steve to have the entire diner recorded at all times, so turning off the alarm system wouldn't stop the video. But Lois didn't need to know. "One, three, one, one, three eight."

Lois' smirk meant Mina would appear to continue her 'cooperation'. If she had to die, at least it would be caught on the system.

Wayne emerged from the walk-in refrigerator's wall, focused on Lois, lip pulled in a snarl, hands balled at his side. He stopped next to her, but didn't try to hit her any more.

Lois's head swung toward him, eyes searching, then turned back to Mina. "Who's here? Is anyone inside? Tell me or I'm going to shoot you." Mina had tried not to look in his direction, but the secretary's agitation seemed to increase by the second. The gun had swung wildly before she'd jabbed it back at Mina to make her point.

Ha. Like Lois wasn't going to shoot her anyway. "No one is here, Lois. Only you and me." And a ghost... But who'd believe it? She suppressed a despairing half laugh. "Why are you doing this? I never did anything to you."

"I told you." Her voice turned cold as a Texas

winter blue-norther. You shouldn't go through people's personal things. That's why I took everything out of my desk and kept the bottom drawer locked after Wayne broke into the church. At least I *thought* I kept it locked." Her fingers tightened around the gun.

Her desk. Mina's mind scrabbled for what she'd seen there. The...pen? The heavy black fountain pen...probably old...and probably donated by Stacey to the auction and was a...a...vintage Montblanc. Lois stole the pen? A danged pen? Wait a minute. She'd mentioned Wayne breaking into the church. Had he blackmailed her, too? Over what?

Wayne, who'd retreated to the corner earlier, came back to start circling the woman. His hands clenched repeatedly.

Mina tried her best to ignore him. "I just needed something to write with, Lois." Mina used her most soothing tone, the one she'd have used with Jake when he skinned a knee on his bike. Since she hadn't been told to keep her hands up, she pushed them out to support her supplication. Wayne started muttering and Mina did her best to shut him out.

Lois's laugh turned maniacal. "As if pretty pleas will help you now. You should've died when you were supposed to."

"Died?" It took a second for the implication to set in. "It wasn't Brian who cut my brakes. You did it."

Lois's smirk confirmed Mina's guess. "Lucky me Chief Ruiz came by looking for Brian yesterday and told me why. God gave me the inspiration and the ability to figure out how through the internet when I discovered what you'd found."

"But why? No one knows you stole the pen."

"You stupid bitch," Wayne screamed. "You were supposed to pay the money and I would've left you alone."

"Good gravy, Wayne, shut up. You're not helping." Oh no. Mina slapped a hand over her mouth.

"Wayne? Where is he?" For a moment, Lois scanned the diner's kitchen, then laughed, the cackling echoed off the tile. "He's dead, you stupid woman. You can't get me to believe he's alive."

Maybe Mina could turn the Flannigan Gift to her advantage. "Wayne's a ghost. He's standing right next to you." She pointed to where he stood, staring at Lois as if he could kill with his eyes. "He was blackmailing you, wasn't he?"

Lois smirked. "How'd you figure it out? Did he tell you he was blackmailing me and my brother? He must have. Who have you told? Your husband?"

Mina's heart slammed painfully against her

chest. "No. I haven't told Garrett. Wayne told me." Wait, Lois's brother?

Another string of profanity emerged from the church secretary. "Stop lying. Now I know your husband has to die."

Desperation drove her to the one person—erm, soul—who'd know how to make Lois believe her. "Wayne."

"What?" he snapped.

"What did you learn about Lois?"

"Stop it," Lois said. "There's not ghost here. I can't see him."

"He's standing right next to you, to your right," Mina said. "Hole on the left side of his chest, right where you shot him."

Wayne folded his arm over his chest, covering much of the t-shirt's blood stain. "She and her good brother were run off from Georgia because they were stealing from the congregation. I found their financial statements. Ask her if she know who Kari Black is."

Mina related Wayne's comments and the question.

Lois sputtered, face turning red. She squeezed the trigger.

THIRTY-TWO

Mina jumped to her right and came up on the far side of the freezer's corner, heart leaping out of her chest. She peeked around the edged from her crouch.

Wayne picked up a small sauce pan from the counter where it had been staged for tomorrow's service. He threw it at Lois and it hit her in the shoulder.

She fired the gun in Wayne's direction, but it wouldn't have done any good. The bullet whizzed off the fryer. "Who's there?" She wheeled the gun around in a frantic arc.

"Ask her if she knows who Donald Black is." Wayne said.

"Who's Donald Black?" Mina screeched.

A bullet whizzed off the tile next to her shoulder. Mina hadn't intended her question to be for the other woman. At this rate, Wayne was going to get Mina killed. She reached behind her for something, anything, as a weapon. She grasped the freezer's door handle. The freezer. She pulled the lever and swung inside, pulling it shut behind her. Pops sounded from outside, each with a metallic thump. She crouched, breath coming from her mouth in white clouds, hanging on to the inside handle with all her might, one foot on the floor, the other bracing it against the hard interior wall. The door opened fractionally with successive tugs, but each time Mina pulled it shut. A couple of more pop-thuds. One sounded a little different and ended with a muffled scream. Mina hung on, praying the door would hold against Lois's bullets.

Then nothing. The tugging stopped. Mina continued to hold the heavy metal panel shut. What could've been hours or only minutes later, a man's voice sounded, indistinct, through the heavy metal and insulation. Mina didn't let up, though her hands had become like ice, she might lose pieces of skin if she had to let go. The tugging started again. Mina pulled harder Someone beat on the door.

"Mina." Deep. Not a female's voice. "Mina. It's okay. You can come out." The lever rattled again.

Garrett. It was Garrett's voice.

She let go of the lever and the door flew open.

She rushed into her husband's arms and hugged him hard, never wanting to let go. His strong arms wrapped around her. She started shivering—from the cold, from the reaction, it didn't matter. Garrett's heat sank into her, warming her heart, her soul. She could've stood there for hours, but a metallic clacking made her lift her lashes.

Two paramedics had lifted a gurney to full height and began to wheel it off. The body strapped atop, handcuffs securing each arm to the metal rails? Lois. A uniformed Dew Drop police officer followed the stretcher as it disappeared down the hallway toward the alley. The woman's eyes had been closed and she hadn't moved or made a sound.

Mina swallowed hard. "Is she dead?"

"No." That had been Daniel's voice.

She shifted in Garrett's arms and found Chief Ruiz leaning against the sink, deep scowl on his face, straw hat tapping against his leg at a rapid pace. She cuddled back into the safety of her husband's embrace, retreating from Daniel's anger.

Silence reigned for several seconds before it became apparent she was supposed to tell him what happened. For obvious reasons, she left out Wayne's appearance and questioning, as well as the names he'd used that had started Lois shooting at her. Garrett didn't comment, just kept those wonderful warm arms around her, giving her the strength to tell her story.

At the end, Chief Ruiz remained quiet for several moments as if digesting her tale and finding it not quite to his taste. "How'd she end up on the floor with a big lump on her head from the pan?" He pointed to the floor, where one of the Cup's well-used cast-iron skillets set. "We found her next to it."

"I have no idea." Surely Wayne couldn't have done it? But he'd moved the smaller pot on the other side of the kitchen. Maybe he could've swung the cast-iron skillet. "I didn't come out until now. Wait. How did y'all know I was here?"

"Dad tried calling you to make sure you made it home. When you didn't answer, he called me. I tried you, then I called Daniel, then I ran down here." It accounted for the heat pouring off of him, then.

"I came over immediately and saw Garrett's truck running," the Chief said. I knocked, called for you, then had to kick in the door. You're going to have to get it fixed." His hand swept out. "Along with all this damage."

For the first time Mina took in her surroundings. The freezer door had multiple large dents in the metal, and an equal number of holes pockmarked the tile around it. Her heart sank. More money for more repairs.

"Insurance should cover it," Garrett said with a gentle, reassuring squeeze. "You're still alive. A freezer door is worth it."

"Is there something you aren't telling me?" The Chief's gaze held a healthy amount of skepticism. "Was there anyone else here?"

"No one else, just me and Lois." And Wayne's ghost. Where had he gone, anyway?

"You sure?"

"Well, you wouldn't believe me if I told you." She continued after Chief Ruiz crossed his arms at his chest. "I think Wayne's ghost was here."

He shifted. "You don't believe in ghosts."

Full monty or no? She decided on partial monty. "Not quite right. I *didn't* believe in ghosts. I didn't want you to think I'm crazy, but that small pan flew from the counter and hit her in the body out of nowhere." With the Chief's skeptical gaze examining the pot, she continued, "I know it sounds crazy, but something was here." She took a chance. "Do the names Kari and Donald Black mean anything to you?"

He's brows crinkled. "Why?"

"I—I heard them and that's when Lois started shooting. I didn't tell you because I know how you feel about paranormal stuff."

"You *heard* them."

"Yeah. In Wayne's voice."

His mouth twisted. "I'll check it out. I'll expect you in tomorrow morning for a statement. In the meantime, get some rest. If you're seeing ghosts, you obviously need a good night's sleep."

THIRTY-THREE

The next afternoon, Olivia used her fork to cut a bite of Mina's new creation, a butterscotch-silk pie topped with a maple whipped cream, made even more indulgent by a generous sprinkle of candied bacon on top. The crust? Graham cracker and toasted pecan. Hopefully, customers would find it to be a slice of fall-flavored heaven.

Mina stopped to take in the rapturous expression on her friend's face with satisfaction. "How is it? I'm a little worried we may be going a bit too far from the standards." Fall loomed around the corner, on the calendar if not on the thermometer yet, and she wanted to get another pie to add to the holiday theme beyond her popular pecan, and the pumpkin with a cinnamon-walnut crunch top.

Olivia swallowed the bite. "Holy moly, lady. This

is fabulous. Sweet, savory, silky soft *and* crunchy. Even if nobody else likes it, this will be the pie you make for November."

About to refill Olivia's glass with sweet tea, Mina stilled. "What?"

"I didn't tell you? I won your pie-a-month at the auction, and this will be my Thanksgiving pie."

"Will do." Mina's heart did a happy dance knowing she'd be making the pies for a friend.

Olivia took a sip from her glass, then smiled slyly. "Looks like Wayne made up for screwing you out of your Ice Tea Festival income. Where else can you get a great meal and hob-nob with the woman who brought down Kari and Donald Black?" She popped another bit of the pie into her mouth with relish.

"I'm ready to fall over, I'm so tired. But I sure am happy for the business." Just to keep her eyes open, Mina swiveled a bit on the red-vinyl clad counter stool in the very back corner.

Olivia pushed a blonde strand back over her shoulder. "I can't believe Lois and Pastor Davis—Kari and Donald Black—were cons going from church to church, stealing what they could, and trusting people's Christian goodness to let them off scot-free so they could do it to someone else."

Maybe the pair were never reported to the police

out of people's goodness. Or maybe those people didn't want to be embarrassed by their lack of a real background check. Mina mentally shrugged. "Worse for Fellowship Church is they hired cons who were also murderers."

The crowd waiting at the door parted and Chief Ruiz strode through. The patrons stopped their low chatter and furtive glances her way to follow him. Too bad he was headed her direction.

Mina slipped off the stool, slid around the counter and popped her head in the service window. "You have the Chief's chicken fried steak up?"

Clara slid it on the ledge with a wan smile. Mina had tried to get her to take the day off, but after her release from Eastland County this morning, the older woman said she hadn't done anything but sleep, so she might as well come in and earn some money.

"Right on time. Thanks."

"You know you don't have to thank me. If you would let me, I'd work for free after all you did." The cook turned away to tend to the fryer which had started beeping.

A little bit of guilt trickled through Mina. If she hadn't been able to talk to ghosts, she wouldn't have poked around in Wayne's murder. But then again, maybe she would have, considering Clara's arrest.

She put the plate in front of Chief Ruiz, who'd sat on the stool she'd been saving for him.

"Thanks, Mina. I didn't have time for breakfast."

"Eat. I'll be back in a minute." She refilled Olivia's glass then made a pass through the diner, water pitcher in one hand, tea pitcher in the other. Several customers stopped her along the way, but she brushed off any suggestions she'd solved the case or that she'd almost been killed, too. "I just got caught in the middle," she'd say then whisk off to the next table.

By the time she'd made it back, Chief Ruiz had demolished his lunch and Olivia's plate contained only her fork and a few spare crust crumbs. "Took longer than I realized." Mina swiped an errant strand of hair from her face and tucked it behind her ear.

The Chief put his fork down with a happy sigh, then focused on Mina. "I know you don't listen to me often, but you need to go home. You've had a busy week, young lady."

More than he could ever imagine. She chuckled. "I'm a little busy *now*, if you didn't notice."

"You are a dead girl walking," Olivia scolded. "You need to go home and spend the rest of the day recouping with your family. You deserve it."

Mina turned to look at the crowded diner as their

words sunk in. It wasn't the first time she'd heard it. Rageena had tried to push her back out the door at eleven when Mina arrived from her making her police statement. She brushed it off. Then Clara chastised her for being there. Then Kayla. And Geri, too. But they were busy, the Cup needed her, right? She tracked each of her employees as they moved through the cafe, plates in hand, bussing, filling glasses, seating people. Though customers still waited at the door, her staff ran the ship like clockwork. She could trust them to keep it working if she took the afternoon off. The realization left her thunderstruck.

"The day after someone tries to kill you, you met with the Rangers for three hours, then you come and work for four hours? Don't make me pick you up and carry you out in front of all these people." The Chief's tone carried amusement, but Mina didn't doubt for a minute he wouldn't do it.

She set the pitchers down and sought her best 'Meanest Girl West of the Mississippi' face. "Okay." She folded her arms across her chest for emphasis.

"You shouldn't argue with Chief..." Olivia's face morphed from stern too incredulous. "Did you say 'okay'?

Mina's humor couldn't be contained any longer and she burst out laughing, joined by her friend and

Chief Ruiz. "Garrett's picking up Jake and it'll be nice to spend the afternoon with them."

The Chief sent her an assessing glance. "Well now that we've settled that, I have one more thing you need to promise me."

"Sure."

"Don't get involved in murder investigations ever again." No sarcasm. No snark. Pure seriousness.

"You got it." The last couple of days must've taken a decade off her life.

Olivia shot a suspicious glance to Chief Ruiz. "She gave in way too easy."

"No kidding." He raised a bushy brow.

"Ha, ha." Mina crossed her heart with an index finger. "I solemnly swear not to get involved in murder investigations. Besides, when would something like this ever happen again? It's Dew Drop, for heaven's sake." She fished her keys out of the front pocket of her jeans shorts. "Now, if you two bossy people will excuse me, I have the two best men in Texas to go spend time with."

Next in the Flannigan Sisters Mysteries
Murder Most Merry!
Available December 3, 2019

Lacey Flannigan should be wallowing in the cheer of her favorite time of the year—Christmas. She just aced finals in her toughest college semester yet. Instead, she's working herself into a frazzle with extra shifts as a vet-tech, a service project at the shelter, and studying for classes that haven't even started yet. Plus, she can barely make time for Walker, the dreamy firefighter she met during summer break who believes in her crazy premonition powers.

But at the shelter's Christmas Save a Pet campaign kickoff, the director tragically dies of a heart attack. Police swoop in claiming that not only is major money missing from the shelter's donations, but they suspect murder. It's bad enough she'd foreseen the director's death before it happened and couldn't stop it—when Lacey becomes the prime suspect in the killing, she must find the real culprit before she spends the holidays behind bars.

Turn the page for an excerpt from *Murder Most Merry*...

Murder Most Merry
CHAPTER ONE

Lacey Mae Flannigan popped the button with her thumb, then slid the reindeer antlers on her head. The little colored lights twinkled back at her in the mirror as promised on the tag. She grinned at her reflection, dabbing on just a bit more lip gloss. A typical day at the San Angelo Animal Shelter wouldn't have qualified for gloss, let alone makeup.

Today, though, a news crew would come for the kickoff of the shelter's Home For The Holidays event. And this morning she'd be the 'elf' who brought in the puppies and kitties for their on-camera chance at finding a loving home for the holidays, just two weeks to the day from now.

She'd gone whole-hog on the dollar-store silly Christmas accessories. Holly earrings dangled from each ear, bells jingled from her wrists and over the ugliest Christmas t-shirt she could find. Bonus? It had cats with Santa hats. A strand of hair had escaped her side ponytail and she tucked it behind her ear. She smiled cheekily at her reflection in the locker room glass. With all the holiday bling on top and her chunky belt's big silver buckle, worn jeans and tall rubber work boots on the bottom, she looked a perfect holiday shelter goofball. Exactly as intended.

Lacey loved the holidays, all of the decorations, the crazy Christmas attire, the music, the sense of family and friends. The only thing missing this time of year was the cold weather and snow. But San Angelo sat squarely in the middle of West Texas, a place not known for its idyllic Christmas wonderland scenery. And today would top the seventies, maybe close to eighty, hence the t-shirt. She'd preferred to wear the truly hideous vintage sweater she'd scouted at the thrift store, but she'd melt in the heat. She shut her locker and turned toward the exit.

Parker Davis pushed through the door and halted two steps in. She propped one hand on a cocked hip and slid her pony-tailed braids back over her shoulder with the other. "Whoa, girl, you went… all out. Sam's gonna have a whole herd of longhorns." In contrast, Lacey's morning-challenged roommate wore one of their San Angelo State Veterinarian Studies t-shirts, stained jeans, and the black rubber boots they all wore to keep their regular shoes from being covered with pee and poo.

"He'll get over it." Lacey grinned and executed a model-ish turn, with a tah-dah ending. "It's not every day you get to be on television. Hey, I have to run and get the animals for their big moment. See ya!"

She pushed through the door and into the vinyl tiled hallway, then took a left into the kennel area.

A chorus of barks greeted her. Some could think it overwhelming, but Lacey always chose to see it as the sound of hope, that the pups still had a chance. She gathered her carriers onto a flat rolling cart, then pulled the list from her back pocket and started down the rows for Nosey, Vixen, and Larry. All three dogs loaded in short order. Lacey wheeled into the cat kennels for Charmin, Smoke, and Opie. The last of the three, the big ginger tabby, purred as she picked him up. She stroked his fur and gave him a little squeeze with a small prayer to the cosmos for luck before she put him in the plastic container. What a love bug. How had he gone for months without anyone wanting him? If her small, two-bedroom apartment that she shared with Parker didn't ban pets, Opie would've gone home with her a long time ago.

She headed back toward the conference room where the news crews would set up. Along the short distance, she passed the lunchroom where her green tea had been steeping in a shelter gimme-mug while she kitsched-out. She ditched the wet tea bag and screwed the silver travel cup's top back on.

Sam Valera stepped in as she headed out, then stopped dead, jaw working a muscle in his cheek. *Oh yay*. He may have been a couple of years younger, but for some reason he thought he knew better than anyone about any subject. His critical brown eyes raked her down, then up, brows joined in an expression Lacey had come to call the Sammy McJudge Special. "Uh, Lacey, what are you wearing? It was supposed to be the Vet Studies t-shirt. You know, to get us some props for volunteering?"

Oy. She shouldn't have needed the Flannigan Gift to know he'd show up. The dude could rival her sister for Control Freak of the Year, especially now since Mina had let up a bit and realized she had her own paranormal powers. Sam put her teeth on edge. "Yeah, well. I guess they're all in the laundry, so I thought I'd wear something festive." She pasted on the hugest fake smile she could muster. Sam could pad his vet school resume for 'helping to coordinate this event' without her.

"You can borrow mine." He reached down and started tugging it from his jeans.

Oh God. Lacey fled from the room with her tea before he could free it from his waistband. She set her mug in a convenient depression on Vixen's crate and pushed, the yucks cruising up and down her back at the prospect of Sam's naked belly. Lacey continued on through the steel double doors into the public area, humming *Jingle Bells on My Boots*, the latest Country Swing Kings release, then pulled to a stop at the conference room. Through the door, Lacey spied a tall man in cargo shorts and a polo shirt setting up a camera on a tripod. Three sets of lights created a kind of triangle flanking the camera. Two upholstered arm chairs set angled toward each other, ready for a conversation, one was already filled with a blonde with her back to the door, the reporter, for sure.

The cameraman spied Lacey. "Are you the director?"

She laughed and stepped up to the doorway. "Not me."

"That'd be me." Cathy Mayfield appeared at Lacey's shoulder. The petite woman's tanned skin looked positively ashen and her glow didn't come from health and her happy nature, more from a fine sheen of perspiration.

"Great, let's get you mic'ed up," the man said.

It took all Lacey could do for her mouth not to hang open. She put her hand on Cathy's arm "You don't look too well." Her eyes flashed to the shelter's Fundraising Chairperson, Sarah Chambers, who'd followed Cathy into the room, hands clasped tightly. "I'm sure Sarah can do this if needed."

"I'm fine," Cathy said, her voice a weak croak, then cleared her throat. "I'm fine, really." A little less husky, but hardly stronger. She drained the shelter-logoed silver travel coffee mug that never seemed to be far from her. A grimace crossed her face as she set the mug next to Lacey's. "Probably just coming down with flu. Things aren't even tasting right. I'll get this interview done and then I'll go home." She entered the conference room.

"Sounds like a good idea," Lacey murmured. Good grief. The woman looked like death warmed over a dozen times. She should be in bed with a flu medication, not infecting the whole shelter staff. Shaking her head, Lacey opened Nosey's carrier and slipped a lead over his neck, then waited next to the door for Sarah's wave to bring him in, just like they'd rehearsed. Maybe sensing her worry, Nosey bumped his snout against her leg with a little whine. Lacey went to one knee and ruffled his ears. "Humans should take better care of themselves," she murmured for his hearing only.

Her senses started tingling and the familiar coldness stole over her. Lacey's allowed the Gift to take over. Sparkles grew in her vision and she closed her eyes, helpless against the vision, it would deliver its information even if she fought it. Her mind floated and her breathing slowed. First colors swirled and sparked, then grainy pictures formed. Cathy drinking from her coffee cup just seconds ago. Cathy sprawled face-down on beige linoleum exactly like the shelter's. They cycled like flashcards, one, two, one, two, over and over.

The scenes faded, as did the grip the Gift held her in. Lacey's eyes popped open and she sucked in a gasping breath. Along with her head pounding as she returned to reality, her heart matched the brutal rhythm. Her hand covered her mouth. No. It couldn't be. She accessed the memories again. Oh no. In both images, the woman's body had been wreathed in a crawling black aura.

Black meant death. If it had been red, she could be saved, but black gave no option. Cathy would die today. From...the flu? Didn't matter. She needed to get to the hospital. *Do what you can for who you can. You can't change what's meant to be.* Gramma's words provided little comfort in times like these.

"Lacey," Sarah hissed, waving her forward through the doorway with frantic hands.

Lacey didn't move at first, torn between bringing Nosey in and running in like a crazy woman and stopping the interview.

Sarah's hand wave became more frantic and her eyes bugged a little.

Lacey's heart pounding like a herd of panicked horses, she guided Nosey into the room between the two seated women as Sarah previously instructed. As she approached, she examined Cathy. If possible, she looked even worse than a bare minute ago when the interview started. Her eyes had turned glassy, and her skin had completely lost color.

"And who do we have here?" the reporter asked. Even for morning news, the woman's cheer seemed over the top and forced.

"Nosey. He's a pit-bull mix. Great with other dogs." Cathy struggled to get just those words out.

She didn't reach for the leash as Lacey had expected to show off the dog. Nosey rolled over at Lacey's feet. She leaned down and rubbed the proffered belly and the pup responded with tongue-lolling, tail-wagging glee. *We need to get this over as soon as possible.* Lacey stood and like magic, Sarah came for the lead, then handed her Vixen. They exchanged glances, Sarah's echoed the worry which had taken over Lacey. But the other woman couldn't know the outcome facing Cathy.

Sometimes Lacey hated the Flannigan Gift. Nerves chewed on her stomach. The woman was fading right before her eyes and she was doing nothing. Lacey stepped forward, 'Stop' trembling on her tongue.

Cathy reached out for Vixen's leash, appearing to rally. Her color appeared a bit better, up one step from battle-ship grey. "I can't believe we still have

Vixen. She's the perfect little miss." She sounded a bit better too.

Lacey sucked back the words hovering on her lips and stepped back. Maybe Cathy wasn't as bad as Lacey feared. The reporter oohed and ahhed over the little dachshund, then it was Larry's turn. The big, dopey guy lumbered in and sat at Lacey's feet looking up at her with the eye of a dog who just wanted affection.

"This is Larry. We think he's a Bloodhound-Labrador mix. Can you stand those ears?" Cathy's color had faded again, words had turned robotic, no trace remained of the dedicated, passionate animal rescue advocate.

Oh no. Lacey's smile may have been wide, but anyone who knew her would recognize it as fake. She played with the long, bunny-soft ears for a moment, earning Larry's signature panting smile of doggo love.

Seeming to understand something was wrong with Cathy, the reporter took control and signed off with a smile.

During the seconds it took, Lacey kept Cathy in her peripheral vision. Breathing, but shallow. The director's hands gripped the chair's wooden arms as if a lifeline.

"And we're off air," the cameraman said.

The director lurched to standing and took a

couple of stumbling steps toward the door. Lacey raced to her and yelled, "Someone call nine-one-one."

Cathy collapsed, sprawled faced down on the beige tile.

Exactly as Lacey had foreseen.

ALSO BY AMANDA REID

Finders Keepers - A Flannigan Sisters Mystery

ABOUT THE AUTHOR

Amanda Reid is an author of light paranormal cozy mysteries, with an urban fantasy series to be released mid-2020. Since she was young, she's been a lover of mystery, sci-fi, romance, and paranormal books. Amanda found her first romance book in her aunt's closet around thirteen years of age and quickly decided it needed to be added to her repertoire. As do many readers, she'd always dreamed of writing. She finally learned the secret, and she'll let you in on it--do it. That simple.

Beyond writing, Amanda was a career Army brat and lived in exotic locations like Tehran, Iran and DeRidder, Louisiana as a child. She obtained an International Politics degree and dreamed of a career in the State Department, but ended up as a federal agent. Amanda spent 24 years investigating murders, fraud, identity theft, drug dealers and many other crimes before retiring in mid-2019. As you can imagine, it's given her a wealth of inspiration for her mystery and urban fantasy stories.

She currently lives in Texas with her husband

and two gonzo Australian Shepherds. Catch up with her on Twitter or Facebook. You can sign up for upcoming releases and promos at amandareidauthor.com.